William Salter

The Life of Henry Dodge

1782 - 1833

William Salter

The Life of Henry Dodge
1782 - 1833

ISBN/EAN: 9783744677875

Printed in Europe, USA, Canada, Australia, Japan

Cover: Foto ©Raphael Reischuk / pixelio.de

More available books at **www.hansebooks.com**

HENRY DODGE,

FROM 1782 TO 1833.

WITH PORTRAIT BY GEORGE CATLIN
AND MAPS OF THE BATTLES OF THE PECATONICA AND
WISCONSIN HEIGHTS IN THE BLACK HAWK WAR.

By WILLIAM SALTER.

BURLINGTON, IOWA:
1890.

HENRY DODGE,

GOVERNOR OF THE ORIGINAL TERRITORY
OF WISCONSIN.

IOGRAPHIES are the life of history. Great men are the chief elements of a nation's power and renown. Plutarch's "Lives" furnish the best account extant of the old Greeks and Romans. He who has mastered the biographies of George Washington, Benjamin Franklin, Thomas Jefferson, Andrew Jackson, and Abraham Lincoln, knows the chief parts of American history. When Thomas Carlyle had completed his "Elucidation of Oliver Cromwell" he wrote to Ralph Waldo Emerson: "I wish you would take an America hero and give us a history of him."

The settlement and growth of the territory northwest of the Ohio river is one of the marvels of American history; it cannot be better told than in the lives of its pioneers. Prominent among them, a heroic man, was Henry Dodge. Born in that territory at Post St. Vincents (Vincennes), October 12th, 1782, his life covered nearly the whole of the first century of its settlement. The Canadian French had been earlier upon the ground, but he was the first "American" child born

in what is now the State of Indiana. He was a leader in
putting an end to the Black Hawk war. One of the results
of that war, "partly as indemnity for the expense incurred,
and partly to secure the future safety and tranquillity of the
invaded frontier," was a cession to the United States of a
tract lying along the west bank of the Mississippi, from which
Black Hawk had gone to wage war in April 1832, and upon
which the next year the first permanent settlements in what is
now Iowa were commenced. He was governor of the original
Territory of Wisconsin, when what is now Iowa was included
therein. A sketch of his life and public services is appropriate
to the IOWA HISTORICAL RECORD.

Among his papers, which were preserved by his son,
Augustus C. Dodge, is a package bearing the simple inscrip-
tion in his handwriting, "Commissions in the Service of My
Country." There was also included in this package the commission of his father, Israel Dodge, as sheriff of the District
of St. Genevieve, signed by William Henry Harrison, governor and commander in chief of the Indiana Territory and of
the District of Louisiana, John Gibson, secretary, October 1,
1804.

The commissions of Henry Dodge cover a long period of
public service. They embrace the signatures of six presi-
dents of the United States, and of many other distinguished
men. It is doubtful if there exists another collection of equal
interest and value in the documentary history of the West, unless it may be in connection with the life of William Henry Harrison, or the life of Lewis Cass, who were illustrious pioneers.
They were not born, like the subject of this memoir, in the
West; but they filled with honor some of its highest stations.

The following is a list of commissions in the package referred to:

1. Lieutenant of Militia in the District of St Genevieve; signed by James
Wilkinson, governor and commander in chief of the Territory of Louisiana;
Joseph Browne, secretary, May 10th, 1806.

2. Adjutant of the Militia in the District of St. Genevieve; signed by

James Wilkinson, governor, etc., July 17th, 1806. This commission also bears the oath of office sworn to by H. Dodge before Jno. Smith, T., March 2d, 1807.

3. First Lieutenant of St. Genevieve Troop of Cavalry; signed by Frederick Bates, secretary of the Territory of Louisiana, and exercising as well the government thereof as the office of commander in chief of the militia of said territory; St. Louis, August 14th, 1807.

4. Captain of St. Genevieve Trooop of Cavalry; signed by Meriwether Lewis, governor and commander in chief of the Territory of Louisiana; F. Bates, secretary, July 10th, 1809.

5. Marshal for the Territory of Missouri; notification of appointment by President Madison; signed by James Monroe, secretary of state, August 10th, 1813.

6. Sheriff of the County of St. Genevieve; signed by William Clark, governor of the Territory of Missouri; F. Bates, secretary, October 1st, 1813.

7. Brigadier General of the Missouri Territory; to rank as such from the 17th of January, 1814; signed by James Madison, president of the United States; J. Armstrong, secretary of war, Washington, April 16th, 1814.

8. Sheriff of the County of St. Genevieve; signed by Wm. Clark, governor of the Territory of Missouri; F. Bates, secretary, September 30th, 1815.

9. Marshal for the District of Missouri; notification of appointment by President Madison; signed by John Graham, chief clerk of the department of state, February 25th, 1817.

10. Marshal in and for the Missouri District for four years; signed by James Monroe, president; John Quincy Adams, secretary of state, April 25th, 1822.

11. Major General of the Second Division Missouri Militia; signed by Alexander McNair, governor of the State of Missouri; Wm. G. Pettus, secretary of state; St. Charles, May 8, 1822.

12. Marshal of the United States in and for the District of Missouri for four years from April 25th, 1826; signed by J. Q. Adams, president; Henry Clay, secretary of state, December 22d, 1825.

13. Chief Justice of the County Court in and for the County of Iowa for four years from December 1st, 1829; signed by Lewis Cass, governor of the Territory of Michigan; J. Witherell, secretary; Detroit, October 14th, 1829.

14. Colonel in the Militia of the Territory of Michigan; signed by Lewis Cass, governor; October 15th, 1829.

15. Major of the Battalion of Mounted Rangers, to rank from June 21, 1832; signed by Andrew Jackson, president; Lewis Cass, secretary of war, June 22d, 1832.

16. Colonel of the Regiment of Dragoons, to rank from the 4th of March, 1833; signed by Andrew Jackson, president; Lewis Cass, secretary of war; May 10th, 1834.

17. Governor of the Territory of Wisconsin for three years from July 3d, 1836; signed by Andrew Jackson, president; John Forsyth, secretary of state; April 30th, 1836.

18. Governor of the Territory of Wisconsin for three years from July 3d, 1839; signed by M. Van Buren, president; John Forsyth, secretary of state; March 9th, 1839.

19. Governor of the Territory of Wisconsin for three years from February 3d, 1846; signed by James K. Polk, president; James Buchanan, secretary of state; February 3d, 1846.

Henry Dodge was of the fourth or fifth generation from Tristram Dodge, one of the original proprietors of Block Island, Rhode Island.[1] His mother, born in Carlisle, Pennsylvania, was a heroic woman, of Scotch-Irish stock. The Hon. Felix Grundy, of Tennessee, was intimately acquainted with her, and "esteemed her as one of the most rarely-gifted and wonderful ladies he had ever met with."[2] Henry Dodge passed his childhood near Louisville, and at Bardstown, Kentucky. At the age of fourteen he joined his father in Upper Louisiana, then Spanish country, but at different periods returned to Kentucky, where at one time he read law in the office of Col. Allen, who was killed at the battle of the river Raisin, January, 1813. For a sketch of his parents, and for other incidents of his early life, the reader is referred to an article upon his mother, entitled, "A Heroine of the Revolution," in THE RECORD for July, 1886, and to an article upon his son, "Augustus C. Dodge," in THE RECORD for January, 1887.

The public life of Henry Dodge commenced as deputy sheriff of the District of St. Genevieve under his father in 1805, and continued until the expiration of his second term as a senator of the United States in 1857, a period of fifty-two years. In addition to holding the offices indicated by the above enumerated commissions, he was a member of the convention that framed the constitution of the State of Missouri in 1820; he was chosen, in July, 1831, a member of the legislative council of the Territory of Michigan to meet at Detroit in May, 1832, but on account of the breaking out of the

---

[1] Tristram Dodge and descendants, by Robert Dodge, New York, 1886, ch. ix.

[2] MS. Letter of Mrs. E. A. R. Linn to A. C. Dodge, May 2d, 1854; Life and Public Services of Dr Lewis F. Linn, pp. 11, 16, 17, 344; Benton's Thirty Years' View, v. 2, p. 485.

Black Hawk war he did not attend; he was delegate to
Congress from the Territory of Wisconsin, 1841–5; and a
senator of the United States from the State of Wisconsin,
1848–57.

In the summer of 1805 Aaron Burr visited the West. He
was at St. Louis in September of that year, and threw out
vague hints of some splendid enterprise in prospect for the
Western country. Whether under feint of an attack upon
Mexico in the interest of the United States he aimed to seat
himself upon the throne of Montezuma, and extend his
empire over the valley of the Mississippi, remains a mystery.
President Jefferson believed that something of that kind was
in his mind; at the same time he compared him to "a crooked
gun whose aim or shot you could never be sure of." [1]

Upon Burr's expedition down the Ohio in the fall of 1806,
Henry Dodge, with his friend John Smith, T., a man
famous for daring adventure, set out to join it. If there was
to be any fighting, they said, they must take a hand. They
proceeded to New Madrid, where Burr was expecting to
meet recruits coming down the Mississippi. Here they were
apprised of President Jefferson's proclamation declaring the
enterprise unlawful; whereupon they sold their canoes, bought
horses, and returned home. They were of Andrew Jackson's
way of thinking, who said, "I hate the Dons; I would delight
to see Mexico reduced; but I would die in the last ditch before
I would see the Union disunited." On reaching St. Genevieve
they found themselves indicted for treason by the grand jury
then in session. Dodge surrendered himself, and gave bail
for his appearance; but feeling outraged by the action of the
grand jury he pulled off his coat, rolled up his sleeves, and
whipt nine of the jurors; and would have whipt the rest, if
they had not run away. He was a tall man, over six feet
high, straight as an Indian, and possessed great strength. [2]

---

[1] Jefferson's Works, v. 5., pp. 28, 68.

[2] Personal Recollections, by John F. Darby, p. 87.

He was one of the original trustees of St. Genevieve Academy, which was incorporated by act of the governor and judges of the Territory of Louisiana, June 21st, 1808. A large stone building was erected upon a hill overlooking the town, that commands a fine view of the bluffs above, of the prairie below, and of the Mississippi sweeping along in the distance. Mann Butler, the historian of Kentucky, was at one time a teacher in this academy. It was in a flourishing condition in 1854-1862, under the control of Hon. Francis A. Rozier.

A few years after the region west of the Mississippi had come into the possession of the United States, ardent to foster American feeling among the inhabitants, he went up to the ruins of Fort Chartres, to obtain a cannon for a celebration of the 4th of July at St. Genevieve. In the previous century the Fort had been a stronghold of the "Illinois Country;" first, under the possession of both sides of the Mississippi by the French, 1720-1765; afterwards of the east side by the English, 1765-1772.[1] It was now a crumbling ruin. He made up a party consisting of his family, Lewis F. Linn, his half brother, Otto Schrader, one of the judges of the territory, and a few others. They embarked upon a sunny morning in June, 1811, on a keel boat, manned by negroes, who propelled it with poles and sweeps. The voyage was slow and laborious, against a strong current, the distance about ten miles. On reaching the fort they picked out from the debris a heavy cannon, of iron; having no levers or hoisting apparatus, night came on before they succeeded in loading it on the boat, when they floated back to St. Genevieve, the full moon rising

---

[1] On a gloomy spring night in 1772 the Mississippi made its last wild leap at the old fort, and swept away the southern curtain and bastions. The troops vacated the place and built Fort Gage, on the bluffs near Kaskaskia, which was headquarters during the remainder of the British occupation. Fort Chartres was never reoccupied. Its walls formed a quarry for the people of the neighborhood, who carried them off stone by stone. The magazine alone remains intact, and lifts its bramble-covered arch amid the modern farm-yard into which the place has been converted.—*Dunn's Indiana, pp. 76, 77.*

brightly over the turbid river. The people of the village welcomed them home, and assisted in unloading and mounting the cannon, and its thunders reverberated in honor of American independence. The same cannon served for patriotic occasions for thirty years, until it burst on the fourth of July, 1840.[1]

Not a few desperate characters infested the frontiers in those days. His duties as sheriff required energy and decision. While in that office he hung two notorious murderers—Peter Johnson, August 3d, 1810, and Charles Heath, March 9th, 1812—on Academy Hill.

On the first day of October, 1811, he and John Scott, afterwards delegate to Congress from the Territory of Missouri, 1817-21, and member of Congress from the State, 1821-27, were seconds in a duel between two prominent citizens of St. Genevieve, Dr. Walter Fenwick and Thomas T. Crittenden, a brother of the distinguished John Jay Crittenden. The duel was fought on a sandbar, Moreau's Island, a few miles below the village, and Dr. Fenwick fell mortally wounded. Dr. Fenwick had no part in the quarrel which led to the duel, but took a brother's place, from whom Crittenden had refused a challenge.

Before war broke out between Great Britain and the United States in 1812, British emissaries had excited the savages upon the frontiers to hostilities against the American settlements. General Harrison had repulsed them at Tippecanoe, November 7th, 1811; but they rallied to the British side in artful combinations under Tecumseh. Among some tribes, however, there was a division of sentiment. The Sacs of Rock river under "General Black Hawk," as the English called him, entered the British service. Some other bands of Sacs and Foxes were friendly to the Americans, and their chiefs went to St. Louis, and tendered aid to the United States. But our Government declined to employ them. Of restless

---

1 Hon. Firmin A. Rozier, in *Fair Play*, St. Genevieve, January 18th, 1885.

nature, the savages could not remain quiet in a time of war. Marauding bands of different tribes, bent on pillage and murder, beset the scattered settlements. In September, 1812, an assault was made upon Fort Madison, the only fort which the United States had erected in what is now Iowa. The "Boone's Lick Settlement," consisting of about 150 families, in what is now Howard and Cooper counties, Missouri, where Daniel Boone had been the earliest adventurer in 1800, and where his son Nathan had commenced the manufacture of salt in 1807, was in a very exposed situation, and suffered frequent depredations. A number of prominent persons in the settlement were killed by the savages.

Upon the call of the governor of the Territory, Henry Dodge took the field. He raised a mounted rifle company at St. Genevieve, and was made major of the Territorial militia, and was subsequently appointed Brigadier General of the militia of the Territory by President Madison. By his courage and skill, having great knowledge of Indian character, he overawed and composed hostile and wavering bands, and carried relief and protection to the frontiers. His half brother, Lewis F. Linn, who had pursued medical studies with Dr. Gault, of Louisville, Ky., accompanied him as surgeon to the troops.

Parts of several tribes belonging on the east side of the Mississippi had been removed at their own request to the valley of the Missouri, that they might be out of the reach of British influence; but they proved perfidious, and were a terror to the settlements. Among them was a band of Miamies (Piankeshaws), which General Harrison had sent west in order to detach them from the Prophet's band. They occupied the region above the mouth of the Osage river. General Dodge conducted an expedition to correct and punish them in the summer of 1814. It consisted of three companies of mounted men; one from Cape Girardeau, one from St. Louis, one from the Boone's Lick Settlement (Capt. Cooper), and sixty-six Shawnees, under Kishkalwa, a Shawnee chief. In making a rapid movement for the purpose of taking the Miamies by surprise, having the Missouri river to cross, the whole command dashed into the rushing stream, and swam their horses to the opposite shore. They found that the affrighted Indians had deserted their village and taken to the woods. On being collected together the Indians gave up their arms, and begged to be spared their lives. Gen. Dodge accepted their surrender, and was making preparations to dispose of them by sending them out of the country. Meanwhile the "Boone's Lickers" had become infuriated against them from finding in their possession and about their persons articles of booty and spoil which they had taken from their kindred and neighbors whom they had plundered and murdered. Word came to the General that there was to be an indiscriminate massacre of all the Miamies. He immediately rode to the spot where they were collected, and found the frightened Indians upon their knees addressing a death-prayer to the Manitou, while the "Boone's Lickers" were in the act of levelling their guns at them. He quickly spurred his horse between the muzzles of the guns and the Indians, and placing the point of his sword to Capt. Cooper's bosom, told him and his men that they could not shoot except through the dead body of their commander. After some angry looks and hard words the Captain demanded his men to desist.

The Miamies expressed the warmest gratitude to Gen. Dodge for saving them from death. They were afterwards conducted in safety to St. Louis, and conveyed to their former home on the Wabash. Long afterwards in narrating the scene to his son Augustus, Gen. Dodge said that he felt more pride and gratification at having saved the lives of his Miami prisoners than he ever did at any triumph upon the field of battle. His magnanimity and firmness of character deeply impressed the friendly Shawnees and Delawares who were in his command. Twenty years after this event, when stationed at Fort Leavenworth as colonel of U. S. Dragoons, he was visited by various Indian chiefs, among others by Kishkalwa, the

Shawnee chief, who had been with his troops in 1814. As the chief came in he embraced and kissed Col. Dodge, to the surprise of his family who were present. Other spectators were deeply impressed as they saw the chief's esteem and affection for his old commander. More than seventy years after the event, a venerable pensioner who had emigrated to California referred with pride to his having been "a soldier under Henry Dodge in the war of 1812."[1]

In July, 1815, Gen Dodge was stationed with a strong military force at Portage des Sioux, on the west side of the Mississippi, a short distance above the mouth of the Missouri, to maintain order and to prevent any collision or surprise among the chiefs and headmen of the Sacs and Foxes, Pottawattamies, Sioux, and other tribes, who were there assembled with Governor William Clark, of Missouri Territory, Governor Ninian Edwards, of Illinois Territory, and Auguste Choteau, of St. Louis, as commissioners of the United States for the purpose of negotiating treaties of peace. His name is appended as a witness to the treaties made with the Teeton and Yancton tribes, July 19, 1815.[2]

After the war he resumed the business of salt-making which his father had commenced at the mouth of Saline river, and was dubbed "Salt-boiler." At one time he was interested in a large and costly establishment with John Scott and Edward Hempstead at Peyroux's Saline. The business was profitable, but as transportation from the Ohio valley was cheapened by steamboats, which first appeared on the Upper Mississippi in July, 1817, prices declined from five dollars a bushel to 75 cents, and he lost all he had made. He also carried on lead mining and smelting at Shibboleth, in what is now Jefferson County, Mo. The only money in the country was Spanish silver dollars. There was no small coin. "I have frequently seen my father," said his son Augustus, "go to a blacksmith

[1] Record, January, 1887, p. 422.
[2] U. S. Statutes at Large, vii, 125, 128.

shop with a bag of silver dollars, and then cut them up into halves, quarters and eighths, for small change. My mother made buckskin pockets in his clothes to carry this fractional currency."

In May, 1820, he was elected by the people of St. Genevieve County a member of the Convention that assembled the following month at St. Louis and adopted a Constitution for the State of Missouri. The Territorial legislature of 1818 had proposed as the northern boundary of the State a line drawn due west from the mouth of Rock river. It is interesting to the people of Iowa, and of Missouri also, after the lapse of seventy years, to read the reasons which were then assigned for that proposition, viz:

> The districts of country that are fertile and susceptible of settlement are small, and separated from each other at great distances by immense plains and barren tracts, which must for ages remain waste and uninhabited. One of the objects in view is the formation of an effectual barrier against Indian incursions by pushing forward a strong settlement at the little river Platte to the west, and on the Des Moines to the north.[1]

The Convention, however, was content with the limits appointed by Congress in the act to authorize the people of Missouri Territory to form a Constitution and State government, approved March 6th, 1820, which fixed the northern boundary at the mouth of the Des Moines river, and west of that river on "the parallel of latitude which passes through the rapids of the river Des Moines." Years afterwards, when that boundary line became a matter of dispute, he gave his testimony in his message to the First Legislative Assembly of Wisconsin Territory, at its second session held in Burlington, Des Moines County, November 7th, 1837, as follows:

> By the act of Congress of 1820 the limits of the State of Missouri were defined; and it was well understood by the members of the convention who formed the constitution of that state that "the rapids of the river Des Moines" were the rapids on the Mississippi, near the mouth of that river.

Ten years later, under date of Dodgeville, December 11th,

---

[1] A. State Papers, Miscellaneous, ii, 557.

1847, he gave the following testimony, which was submitted to the Supreme Court of the United States in the case of the State of Missouri vs. The State of Iowa:

I was a member of the convention that formed the constitution of the State of Missouri in 1820, and during the session of the convention I never understood or heard the rapids in the river Des Moines mentioned to the best of my recollection; and my recollection is clear in 1820 that the lower Mississippi rapids was called "the rapids of the river Des Moines," or "the river Des Moines rapids."

It was a pleasing incident in his capacity as Major General of the militia of Missouri, to receive the Marquis de Lafayette, and do him military honor upon his visit to St. Louis, the 29th of April, 1825.

Embarrassed in his fortunes, Mr. Dodge left Missouri, in 1827, for the Fevre river lead mines. That region was then attracting the adventurous and the enterprising. He reached Galena at the time of a threatened outbreak of the Winnebago Indians, which had alarmed the settlers. He was called upon by Henry and Jean P. B. Gratiot and other prominent citizens to take the lead in the defense of the district. Many had fled into Galena for safety. "The little place" says an eye-witness, "was crowded with families pouring in from the mines. The flat between the bluff and the river was covered with wagons, families camping in them; block houses were erected on the hill, companies forming, drums beating, and General Dodge busily engaged in organizing troops and creating order and confidence out of terror and confusion." [1]

Gen. Dodge sent Moses Meeker to induce the Fox Indians, who then possessed the country where is now the city of Dubuque, to take sides against the Winnebagoes, but they declined any part in the contest.

The following letter was addressed to Brigadier General Atkinson, U. S. Army, who had come up to the scene of disturbance from St. Louis with a force of 600 infantry and 150 mounted men:

---

1 Mrs. Adele P. Gratiot, Wisconsin His. Collections, x, 270.

Gen. H. Atkinson, Prairie du Chien.

Dear General:—Capt. Henry, the chairman of the committee of safety, will wait on you at Prairie du Chien before your departure from that place. He is an intelligent gentleman, who understands well the situation of the country. The letter accompanying Governor Cass's communication to you has excited in some measure the people in this part of the country. As the principal part of the efficient force is preparing to accompany you on your expedition up the Ouisconsin, it might have a good effect to send a small regular force to this part of the country, and in our absence they might render protection to this region. I feel the importance of your having as many mounted men as the country can afford, to aid in punishing those insolent Winnebagoes who are wishing to unite, it would seem, in common with all the disaffected Indians on our borders. From information received last night, some straggling Indians have been seen on our frontiers.

Your friend and obedient servant.   H. DODGE.

With his mounted volunteers, 130 in number, Gen. Dodge, marched to the Wisconsin river, one detachment going to Prairie du Chien, the other to English Prairie, now Muscoda. They scoured both sides of the river to the Portage, driving the Indians before them, taking one prisoner, a lad of fifteen, who had become separated from his band, and was surrounded. He was son of a chief, Winneshiek, whose name he bore. He refused to surrender, but sat on his horse, with cocked gun in hand. The soldiers were about to shoot him when Gen. Dodge, admiring the intrepidity of the boy, rode up and wrenched his gun from him, and saved him from the death he defied.

Upon reaching the Portage they found that Red Bird and his accomplices in murder had been surrendered to Major Whistler. Decorah, in presence of General Dodge, disclaimed unfriendliness on the part of the Winnebagoes to the United States, and disavowed connection with the murders that had been committed on the Mississippi. Terms of settlement were arranged by Gen. Atkinson, whereupon the volunteers were discharged and returned to their homes.

The disturbance over, Henry Dodge immediately engaged in " prospecting" the country for lead mines, and on the 3d of November, 1827, established himself near the present village of Dodgeville, in what is now Iowa County, Wisconsin. It was the happy hunting grounds of the Winnebagoes, a land of bubbling brooks and crystal springs, of beautiful oak openings, groves of larger timber, and rolling prairies, with a broad ridge separating the waters that flow to the Wisconsin from those flowing to Rock river. It was in that part of the old Northwest Territory (1787), and of the Illinois Territory (1809), lying north of the State of Illinois, which had been attached to the Territory of Michigan upon the admission of the State of Illinois into the Union (1818). Some "diggings" had previously been worked by the Indians, who excavated down an inclined plane, carrying in wood for fuel, heating the rocks, then slacking them with water; charcoal and lime were found in the old works, as also buck-horns which had been used as tools. He made friendly terms with the Indians of the neighborhood, and gave them presents as in the way of rent for occupying their lands. He made a home for his family, and took precautions for their protection and safety. More than a hundred miners soon gathered to the "camp." The neighborhood resounded with the stroke of the ax and the click of tools. Shafts were sunk in every direction. He discovered the only lode in the region that proved to be of much value.

It was not long before complaints were made to the United States Indian Agent, at Prairie du Chien, Joseph M. Street, that white men had invaded the country of the Winnebagoes. He reported the matter to the superintendent of Indian affairs at St. Louis (Gen. William Clark), under date of January 15th, 1828, as follows:

Gen. Dodge with about fifty men, well armed with rifles and prepared for any event, is near the English Prairie on a northern branch of Rock river, called Piketolika, beyond the lands subject to reservations under the treaty of August 24th, 1816. My information is that the Bear, a Winnebago chief, with a few followers are at the place, and have sold the privilege to Gen. Dodge. Many are flocking to him from Fever river, and he permits them to join upon paying certain stipulated portions of the original purchase. The ore is more abundant, nearer the surface, and obtained with greater facility than ever known in this country. It is said that he has raised about half a million of mineral, smelted from 900 to 1000 bars, and is smelting fifty bars a day. With two negro men in one place he raises about 2000 pounds per day. What will be the effect of these high-handed measures I am at a loss to say. Should the tribe disapprove of the bargain of the Bear with Gen. Dodge, mischief might ensue. The cupidity of the Indians may also be awakened, and serious difficulties thrown in the way of any contemplated purchase of this section of the country by our Government. Should his removal as a precautionary measure be recommended, I have no force adequate to the accomplishment of the object, and from a conversation with the commanding officer of the fort here,[1] a sufficient number could not be prudently detached for the purpose.

As far as the most active enquiries and acute observation enable me to judge, the Winnebagoes are quietly pursuing their winter's hunt.

On the 26th of January, 1828, the agent wrote that there were mutterings of discontent among the Winnebagoes; that upon that day a chief (Carumna, the Lame) had said to him:

We promised not to interrupt the white people at the Fever river mines. Then they were digging near the line: now a large camp has gone far into our country, and are taking lead where it is easy to be got, and where Indians have been making lead many years. We did not expect this, and we want to know when this will stop. The hills are covered with them; more are coming and shoving us off our lands to make lead. We want our Father to stop this before blood may be shed by bad men. You tell us our Great Father is a great chief, and has warriors like the sands on the river side, and that the Winnebagoes ought to be at peace with him and his people; that if they kill his white children he will go to war with them, and when they are all killed by his great warriors he will take their country. It would be better with the Winnebagoes then, than to live and see white men come and take their lands while they are living."

I told him their Great Father lived a long way off; that he would remove those white men when it was told him, if they kept their promise and remained at peace. He said: "Well; they would keep their promise."

The same day the agent sent John Marsh, a sub-agent, to notify Gen. Dodge that he must move off instantly, or he would be removed by military force. In a communication of February 7th, 1828, Mr. Marsh reported as follows:

In obedience to your instructions of the 26th ult., I ascended the Wisconsin to the English Prairie, and thence southwardly up the valley of a small river which comes in at that place, and arrived at the residence of Gen. Dodge on the evening of the fifth day after my departure. Your letter to Gen. Dodge I delivered immediately, and I informed him and others who were located in that vicinity that I had a communication to read to them from the Indian agent

---

[1] Major John Fowle, 5th U. S. Infantry.

at Prairie du Chien. The next morning I read your notice to all the principal miners. Not being able to discover any indications of an intention to remove out of the Indian country, your address was also read and the extracts from the treaty therein referred to.

Gen. Dodge addressed the people, and explained to them his views of the subject He insisted principally that there was no definite line of demarcation between the lands of the Winnebago Indians and those of the Chippeways, Pottawattamies and Ottaways of the Illinois, on which the citizens of the United States had a right to dig for lead ore, and that until such line should be definitely marked and established it was by no means certain that the place where they were was on the lands of the Winnebagoes.

The remainder of the day was spent in examining the country. Ore is found in great abundance near the surface, and in large masses. Few of the excavations are more than ten feet deep. The whole country appears to be literally full of lead ore, and the labor of obtaining it is trifling. Traces of old Indian diggings are found throughout the country for several miles. There are also furnaces where the Indians smelted the ore.

Gen. Dodge resides in a small stockade fort near the principal mine. There are about twenty log houses in the immediate vicinity, besides several more remote. He has a double furnace in constant operation, and a large quantity of lead in bars and in the crude state. From the best information I have been able to obtain there are about one hundred and thirty men engaged in mining at this place, and completely armed with rifles and pistols. I was also informed that there about fifteen Winnebagoes ten or twelve miles distant who frequently visit the mines, and who have been presented by Gen. Dodge with several hundred dollars worth of provisions and merchandise. When about to return, I was desired by Gen. Dodge to inform you that he should leave the country as soon as he conveniently could.[1]

Immediately upon the receipt of this communication Gen. Street called upon the commanding officer at Fort Crawford for a detachment of one hundred and eighty troops to remove the trespassers, who replied that as he had only 147 men in

---

[1] To other parties Gen. Dodge is reported as saying that he would leave if Gen. Street had more guns than he had. The same year Morgan L. Martin made an expedition through the mining region, and speaking of it after a lapse of fifty-nine years said: "Our first objective point was Dodgeville, where Henry Dodge had started a "diggings." We found his cabins surrounded by a formidable stockade, and the miners liberally supplied with ammunition. The Winnebagoes had threatened to oust the little colony, and were displaying an ugly disposition. Dodge entertained us at his cabin, the walls of which were well covered with guns. He said that he had a man for every gun, and would not leave the country unless the Indians were stronger than he." Wis. His. Coll. xi. 397.

his command, and but 130 of them were fit for duty, it would be out of his power to comply with the request. Arrangements were soon in progress by the Government for the purchase of the lands of the Winnebagoes. Provisional articles of agreement were made by Gov. Cass and Pierre Menard, commissioners on the part of the United States, with chiefs of the Winnebago tribe, at Green. Bay, August 25th, 1828. In prospect of those arrangements Henry Dodge held his ground, and was unmolested. He had built the first smelting furnace erected by the whites north of the Illinois state-line. He was present at Prairie du Chien, with Henry Gratiot, Antoine Le Claire, Zachary Taylor, and other witnesses to the treaty, under which the Winnebagoes sold their lands in the mining district to the United States, August 1st, 1829.

From Helena on the Wisconsin river, he shipped lead on flat-bottomed boats to New Orleans. Others reshipped on steamers at St. Louis; he was the only one who made the entire voyage without transfer. The trip took three months and a half, and involved peril and hardship.

In the first settlement of the mining country, those who obtained permits to mine were not allowed to cultivate the soil, so that for several years provisions were scarce, and the expense of living was great. When the lands were brought into market, he became the purchaser of more than a thousand acres, and here was his home for nearly forty years. He took part in a patriotic celebration of the 4th of July, and served as President of the Day, in 1829, at Mineral Point, where a discovery of copper had awakened an excitement and called many miners to the place. Upon the organization of Iowa county, the same year, under an act of the Legislative Council of Michigan Territory, setting off that part of Crawford county lying south of Wisconsin river, he was elected chief justice of the county, with Wm. S. Hamilton and James H. Gentry, associate justices, and held the first court in that county.

The growth of the mining settlements, and their distance

from the seat of Government at Detroit, the irregular routes of travel then pursued making it from 800 to 1000 miles, as stated by Gen. Dodge, created a demand for a new territorial organization. The business relations of the miners were with Illinois and Missouri and the General Government, not with the peninsula of Michigan; nor was it to be expected that a delegate elected from the peninsula should understand the wants of a people so remote and detached as they were. He opened a correspondence upon the subject with the delegate to Congress (Austin E. Wing), and laid before him a statement of the inconveniences and hardships under which the people were laboring, and their claims on the National Legislature for the division of the Territory. Under date of Dodgeville, February 10th, 1829, he said·

Laws should be made to suit the condition of the people over whom they are to operate; hence the necessity of a local legislation following a division of the Territory. Another strong reason why we should be separated from the Territory of Michigan is: We are surrounded by Indians, some friendly, others still hostile to the extension of the American empire and to the people of this country. A local legislature and a separate government here would place the people in a situation to defend themselves, and have the aid of the constituted authorities near them. It would be almost impossible to receive aid from the peninsula of Michigan. Mounted companies of riflemen would be the best arm of defence to afford this country protection. Recent events at Rock Island prove the secret influence that exists over the minds of the Indians;[1] and I have no hesitation in saying that so long as that influence exists we will have occasional difficulties with the Indians of our borders.[2]

A bill was reported in Congress, January 6th, 1830, to establish the Territory of Huron, with boundaries embracing what now constitutes the states of Wisconsin, Iowa, Minnesota, a part of the Territory of Dakota, and the upper peninsula of Michigan, but it did not become a law. A somewhat similar bill passed the House of Representatives in 1831, but not the Senate.[3]

---

1 "The secret influence" came of the communication which the "British band" of the Sacs, who were in arms against the United States in the war of 1812, still kept up with Canada. Their chiefs were in the habit of visiting Canada, and were laden with presents on their return.

2 His. of Wisconsin, by W. R. Smith, i, 430–432.

3 History of Wisconsin Territory, by Moses M. Strong, p. 187.

On the 11th of July, **1831**, Henry Dodge was elected to **the Fifth** Legislative Council of Michigan Territory from the counties of Michilmacinac, Brown, Crawford, Chippewa and Iowa. His views of public **duty** at the time were given **in a letter addressed to the electors.**

JULY 8th, 1831.

My name being before the public as one of those who have been nominated by a meeting of citizens at Green Bay as well as at Mineral Point to represent the people of the Seventh Electoral District in the Legislative Council of the Territory, I consider it a duty I owe the electors as well as myself to state explicitly my views in relation to such measures as have for their object the public good, and the course I will pursue if honored with the confidence of my fellow citizens.

The wants and condition of the people west of Lake Michigan in my opinion require a speedy division of the Territory and the establishment of a local legislature. Laws then can be made suited to the manners, habits, and condition of the people residing within the limits of the contemplated territory The relation we stand to the General Government makes it important to us that we should have a direct representation at Washington. Living on the United Stands lands and working their lead mines, it becomes a matter of much interest to the people of the mining country that the rights of pre-emption should be secured to them on the most liberal principles both for the farms they occupy as well as their mineral grounds.

The General Government by its own act has invited the people of the mining country to immigrate to this country for the express purpose of making lead. They are neither squatters nor intruders on the public lands. By their enterprise and industry they have fully realized the views of the Government. The people of the United States have had an abundant supply of lead made, and sold to them cheaper than the manufacturer here could afford to make it. The people of the mining country have paid a greater tax, and that directly upon the labor of the whole community, than any equal number of citizens of the United States, and consequently have stronger claims upon the justice and liberality of the Government than any equal number of citizens who have settled on the frontiers.

Should I be the choice of the electors, on all local subjects the expressed wishes of a majority of the people will govern me. I consider the representative bound in his individual capacity to do what the people would do in their collective capacity, could they be present.

Mr. Martin has been recommended to the people of this electoral district for the Council. He has the reputation of being a young man of talents and integrity.[1] It appears desirable to insure success in our election that we should

---

1 Hon. Morgan Lewis Martin, of Green Bay; he died Dec. 10, 1887. To his efforts Iowa owes the organization of the original counties of Des Moines and Dubuque, under an act of the Legislative Council of Michigan Territory to

cordially unite with Brown county   Mr. Wing is before the people as a candidate for the Delegacy to Congress. The course he pursued when in Congress, in advocating a division of the Territory, was such as the condition of the people required. As he truly represented our interests on a former occasion, it would seem we might safely **trust** him again.

I have been thus explicit **that** my fellow-citizens may know my **views on** all **subjects which I** consider of **interest to** them, not with a view to **influence** them in any way; **it** is the right of every freeman to judge and act for **himself; whatever that decision** may be as it respects myself, I shall cheerfully acquiesce in.

The next winter, in behalf of the people of the mining region he prepared a memorial addressed to Hon. Lewis Cass, Secretary of War, as follows:

The **undersigned residents** of that part **of the** Territory **of** Michigan in-**cluding the lead mine district** on the Upper **Mississippi respectfully** ask leave **to call your** attention to the situation and conditions of the citizens occupying the mineral region.

In **conformity to** an act of Congress passed in 1807, **the president of the United States from** time **to time** has appointed **agents invested with ample powers to lease the** United States **lead mines. The** government of the **mines having been confided to** the War Department, and the rents accruing **to the United States from working these mines having been** regulated by that depart-**ment, is the reason why your memorialists ask** leave to call your attention to **this subject.**

Your **immediate predecessor** in **office having reduced** the rents of **the** United **States mines from** 10 **to 6 per cent, we take it for** granted that power

lay off and **organize counties west of the Mississippi river, approved** September 6th, 1834. **In a letter to A. C. Dodge, of May** 25th, 1883, he recalled "**the rude log cabin in** Dodgeville where **Hon. Lucius** Lyon and **myself were hospitably** entertained, in 1828 **by your excellent** parents. **It seems like a dream. I recognize the** portly Roman, **the** saintly wife, the **stalwart lads and modest daughters,** comprising **the** household, protected **in their well-armed fortress (block house) from the** dangers incident to frontier life; **and from that early period note the wonderful** metamorphosis which time has wrought **in the West. I recall also the erect figure and** proud bearing of your father **when he volunteered to guide us on** horseback to the recent discoveries of copper **ore at Mineral Point, and to the** pits and shafts in the vicinity of Dodgeville, **from which his supply of lead** ore was hauled to his **furnaces,** the athletic figures **of your brother** and yourself, youths of **some** fifteen or eighteen, laboring about the smelting works with **others engaged** around the premises. **Nor can I** forget the appearances of the **negro** slaves, who clung to **your** father's family **even after they were** given freedom, as dutiful children dependent for protection **and daily wants** upon a parent."—*Semi-Centennial of Iowa, at Burlington, pp. 87, 88.*

was properly exercised; and, inasmuch as he held himself at liberty to raise the rents by giving three months' notice, we ask your indulgence while we briefly state the past and present condition of the mining population.

The relation in which you stood as the executive of this Territory at the time his mining country was settled, as well as the appointment you held with Col. Menard as joint Commissioners on the part of the United States for treaty with the Winnebago and other tribes of Indians, gives you a general knowledge of the condition in which the people settled here. It is well known that the Government of the United States invited the people to this country through their agents at a time when they had no troops on this frontier to afford them protection. In 1827, when the Indians commenced hostilities, the inhabitants being wholly dependent on themselves for protection abandoned their mining operations, and prepared themselves to resist the Winnebago Indians who were located in the immediate vicinity of the mines, and who were actually at war. The loss of one season from working the mines, and the expenses incurred by the people during the winter of 1827-8, left them without the means of returning whence they had emigrated. In this situation they settled that portion of the mining country which they now occupy. In June, 1828, the Superintendent of the United States lead mines located that portion of country at that time occupied by your memorialists, and from that period until the extinguishment of the Indian title at Prairie du Chien, in 1829, a period of nearly fourteen months, and before the Government acquired a right from the Indians for the country, the people of the mining country paid upwards of a million pounds of rent lead. It is believed that no tax was ever more punctually and cheerfully paid by smelters to the Government. During the administration of the present Superintendent—two and a half years—more tax lead has been collected, including arrearages, than the actual rents amounted to for that period. Your memorialists state with confidence that they have paid a greater amount of taxes, and that a direct tax on the labor of the whole community, than any equal number of citizens since the settlement of America; that from 1827 until 1829 the smelters not only paid ten per cent on all lead manufactured, but hauled the rent-lead a distance from forty to sixty miles to the United States deposit, at a time when lead was not selling for more than one dollar and fifty cents at the United States lead mines. What was the consequence? The entire ruin of many of the manufacturers. The Government of the United States received between three and four millions of pounds of rent-lead, and the people of the United States an abundant supply of the article of lead upon cheaper terms than at any preceding period. The low and depressed price of lead was the principal cause, no doubt, that your predecessor reduced the rents of the mines, and as the Government has derived all the advantages that could have been anticipated in a national point of view from the exploration and working their mines, and as the manufacturers and miners have not had time to realize the advantages resulting from a reaction in the price of lead, your memorialists confidently rely on your justice and the liberality of the Government, that they will foster and protect their own manufacturers of lead, to the exclusion of those of foreign powers; and as lead is a necessary article in time of war, we trust you will carefully examine the subject in all its bearings before you increase the rent of the lead mines, and that you will urge upon Congress the justice and propriety of not changing the present tariff on lead.

Your memorialists ask leave to call your attention to a subject of great interest and vital importance to them. Should the Government pass a law for the survey and sale of the United States lead mines of this country upon the same principles observed in the sale of their mines in Missouri, we earnestly hope you will recommend to the consideration of Congress the justice and propriety of granting to each miner who has complied with the regulations made for the government of the mines the privilege of working out all discoveries made on mineral lots or surveys. To sell the mines without making this reservation would deprive the most enterprising and industrious part of the population of their all. Miners who have had mineral lands in their possession for years might have them purchased by speculators, and be left without resource or means, from not having had time to compensate themselves for the low prices of mineral, which sold in this mining country for two years from five to eight dollars per thousand pounds.

Your memorialists consider it fortunate for them that you are placed at the head of the War Department of the Government, knowing that you are intimately acquainted with all the circumstances attending the settlement of the mining country, surrounded as they have been by Indians secretly hostile to the American people as well as under the influence of the English; and the friendly regard you evinced for the protection and safety of the citizens of this mining region in 1828 is remembered with gratitude. Your memorialists confidently believe you will render them all the aid in your power consistent with the relation you stand to the government.

To further the objects of this memorial, he also addressed letters to a number of members of Congress of like tenor with the following:

DODGEVILLE, MICHIGAN TERRITORY, January 26th, 1832.

Hon. Elias K. Kane,
        United States Senator from Illinois,
                Washington City:

The interest you have heretofore taken in this remote part of the Territory of Michigan, as well as the particular situation of this country, is the reason I take the liberty of addressing you at this time.

The people of the mining country require the fostering protection of the General Government. They have not had time since the favorable reaction of the price of lead to compensate themselves for their losses. A reduction of the present tariff on the importation of foreign lead would completely destroy the prospects of the manufacture of lead in this country. Great as the diversity of opinions appears to be on the tariff, it would seem that as lead is a necessary and important article in peace and in war the National Legislature should examine the subject in all its bearings before they change the tariff on lead.

The people of this remote region are greatly interested in a division of the Territory during this session of Congress. Our relations being entirely with the General Government, and the great distance we are from the seat of Territorial Legislature, place the inhabitants here in a most unpleasant situation. We have two Councillors elected from five counties. The distance we are from Detroit, and having but two representatives out of thirteen which forms the Council, makes the representation west of Lake Michigan merely nominal. The rapid growth of the peninsula of Michigan, and the interest the people have in becoming a state as early as possible, would give us but a feeble voice in the Council; and however talented and zealous the Delegate from Michigan may be in representing truly the condition of the people here, it is impossible from the distance he resides from us that he can understand well the condition of this country. We want a local Legislature here, where laws can be enacted suited to the condition of the people. Laws are enacted six months before they reach us, and laws enacted for the peninsula of Michigan do not suit our condition.

Another strong reason why we should be severed from Michigan is, we are surrounded by Indians, some friendly, others secretly unfriendly to the American people and jealous of the growth of the country. Should they attack us, we could derive no advantage from the constituted authorities of Michigan, but would have to depend on ourselves for protection. It is true the United States have troops on our borders, but we might be taken by surprise, and the settlements entirely destroyed before they could give us aid. We want the constituted authorities near us, and a proper force of mounted riflemen or gunmen, who could be brought together at the shortest notice. This country is well adapted to the horse service, and they are able to act promptly and efficiently. We are one of the most exposed frontiers of the United States and should be entitled to those rights and privileges which have been extended to others on the frontier.

The particular condition of the people of this detached territory of the United States must make my apology for the length of this communication.

I am, dear sir, with sentiments of the greatest regard,

Sincerely and truly your friend,

H. DODGE.

———

NOTE.—Lyman C. Draper, L.L.D., of Madison, Wisconsin, has kindly furnished the following additional information as to the campaign of General Dodge up the Missouri river in 1814, from personal reminiscences given to him by General Dodge in 1855:

There had been considerable mischief done by the Indians at the Boone's Lick settlement, where, among others, a man who was a potter by trade had been killed; and being the only person of that trade in the region his loss was seriously felt. The settlement was too weak to strike any effectual blow in turn. General Dodge, then of St. Genevieve, who had been appointed by President Madison the successor of Gen. William Clark in command of the militia, when the latter was made Governor of Missouri Territory, waived his rank as General, and took the command as Lieut. Colonel of mounted men, under orders of Brigadier General Benjamin Howard, U. S. Army, to march to the relief of the Boone's Lick settlement, in September, 1814.

The command consisted of 350 mounted men, under Capt. John W. Thompson, of St. Louis, Capt. Isaac Van Bibber, of Loutre Lick, Capt. Henry Poston, of the Missouri Mining Region, Sarshall Cooper, of the Boone's Lick settlement, and Capt. Daugherty, of Cape Girardeau. Nathaniel Cook (now, 1855, aged and blind, of Potosi, Mo.) and Daniel M. Boone were the Majors; and Ben. Cooper, of the Boone's Lick settlement, a veteran of the Indian wars of Kentucky, was along; and Gen. Dodge, having some blank commissions with him, appointed him a Major, wishing him to serve on account of his experience. He was an elder brother of Capt. Sarshall Cooper. David Barton, afterwards the celebrated U. S. Senator of Missouri, was a volunteer in Thompson's company, refusing any rank, only tendering Gen. Dodge any services he might render in the way of aiding him in writing.

There were also about forty friendly Shawanoes along, under four war captains,—Na-kour-me, Kish-Kal-le-wa, Pap-pi-qua, Wa-pe-pil-le-se, the two latter were fully seventy years old, and had both served in the early Indian wars against Kentucky.

This force crossed the Missouri from the northern to the southern bank at the Arrow Rock by swimming the stream. Gen. Dodge selected six of his most active men, good swimmers on horseback, for the advance; the others followed, flanked by canoes, and in the rear by canoes, as a vanguard above and below the main body, stemming the swift current. When about half way over they struck the strong eddy, which soon wafted them to the southern bank in safety. Two hours were consumed in crossing the river with the horses, baggage, etc.

The friendly Shawanoes found and reported the locality of the hostile Miamis, who had thrown up a small fort. Dodge's men pushed forward several miles up the river, and in the night neared the enemy in what is now known as the Miami Bend, in Saline County, and soon surrounded them. Ascertaining this fact, the Miamis, knowing it would be folly to resist such odds, proposed, through the Shawanoes, to surrender themselves as prisoners. Gen. Dodge called a council of his officers, and asked their advice, commencing with the Coopers and other Boone's Lick officers. They all advised receiving them as prisoners, and that their lives must be sacredly preserved. Gen. Dodge told the officers that he should hold them personally responsible for their own conduct and that of their men in this particular.

The Indians now formally surrendered, 31 warriors, and 122 women and children, 153 in all.

The next morning, while Capt. Cooper and others were scouring around in search of hidden property, the Captain found the well known rifle of the poor potter slain in the Boone's Lick region; and in rage he came galloping to Gen. Dodge, and demanded the surrender of the Indian who had murdered the potter, to make an example of him. Gen. Dodge peremptorily declined, when Cooper threatened in behalf of his company, who were dashing up on their horses, to kill the whole of the Indians; and his men as by common consent cocked their rifles in shooting attitude. The Indian warriors seeing the threatening aspect threw themselves upon their knees, and, crossing their breasts rapidly and repeatedly, uttered earnest prayers to the Great Spirit, or rather to the sun, then just rising in its morning splendor. Gen. Dodge, hearing the clicking of the locks of the rifles of the Boone's Lick men, and fearing the consequences, but without ever turning towards them, drew his sword, and thrust its point within six inches of Capt. Cooper's breast, and, reminding him of his pledge to protect the Indians in their surrender, said that he would never consent to their being slaughtered in cold blood, and that if Cooper's men fired on them Capt. Cooper himself should instantly suffer the consequences.

At this critical moment, Major Daniel M. Boone came dashing up to Gen. Dodge's side, and said that he would stand by him to the last; and he taunted Cooper with the treachery of the act he proposed. Dodge was firm, never taking his eye from Cooper's. Boone presented a determined countenance, as brave men always do when actuated by noble purposes. At length Cooper yielded, and Dodge ordered him to take his place in the line, and march away. He doggedly obeyed, and his men rode by. The Indians now jumped to their feet with expressions of joy and gratitude to Dodge and Boone. The Shawanoes, too, were much gratified that the Miamis were spared.

Kish-Ka-le-wa visited Gen. Dodge at Fort Leavenworth, in 1835, and recognized his old commander.

Gen. Dodge looks back upon his conduct in saving these prisoners as one of the happiest acts of his life.

II.

IN THE BLACK HAWK WAR, 1832.[1]

The Black Hawk War was the immediate occasion of the opening of Iowa to civilization in 1833. Had Black Hawk been content to have staid in peace upon his lands west of the Mississippi, he would not have been disturbed there, at least for a number of years; probably not during his life-time. It was his invasion of Illinois that cost him Iowa, as often in grasping another's men lose their own. That war also hastened the settlement of Northern Illinois, which it was intended to prevent, and also the settlement of what is now Southern Wisconsin, as it led immedi-

---

[1] Of the many accounts of the Black Hawk war, the most clear and reliable are by John A. Wakefield and Albert Sidney Johnston. The copy of the History of the Black Hawk War by Wakefield in the Library of the State Historical Society of Wisconsin was presented by the author to James G. Edwards, the founder of the Burlington *Hawk-Eye*. Chapter III of the Life of General Johnston contains valuable portions of the journals he kept at this time.

ately to treaties with the Winnebagoes and Pottawattamies, under which those tribes agreed to leave the lands they had long possessed lying between Lake Michigan and the Mississippi river. The fact that some of those Indians had sympathized with Black Hawk, and had fought under him, intensified the demand that those tribes should be removed. It is thus a historic fact that the founding of the states of Wisconsin and Iowa, and of the city of Chicago, would have been delayed an uncertain number of years, but for the Black Hawk war.

Conspicuous among those who were most efficient in securing these results was Henry Dodge. He was entitled to the honor assigned him in his life time, as a "captain of aggressive civilization." It is the object of this paper to give a narrative of his part in that war.

In April, 1832, information reached the mines that Black Hawk had crossed the Mississippi into the State of Illinois, in violation of stipulations made with him by Gen. Gaines on the 30th of June, 1831, and that he was upon the war path. There were fears and rumors that the Winnebagoes of Rock River and the Pottawattamies of the country about the head waters of Illinois River and about Chicago, would join him. Henry Dodge at once called the miners together at Mineral Point. They deemed it prudent to send a messenger to Rock River, for the purpose of ascertaining the situation, and to learn the strength and purposes of Black Hawk. Daniel Morgan Parkinson, who came to the mines in 1827, and was one of the first settlers at Mineral Point, was chosen for the service. He took dispatches from Henry Dodge to Henry Gratiot, the U. S. sub-Indian Agent for the Winnebagoes, and to John Dixon, who was a friend of the Sacs and Foxes, at Dixon's Ferry. On this errand Mr. Parkinson learned that Black Hawk came to the Prophet's village on the 28th of April with his warriors in battle array, and marched to Mr. Gratiot's lodge, where the neutral flag was flying, and took it down and hoisted the British colors, and treated Mr. Gratiot as a prisoner, until he was ransomed by his clerk, George Cubbage,[1] or Black Hawk was propitiated, with ten plugs of tobacco; and that in reply to a "talk" sent by Gen. Atkinson, advising the hostile chiefs, to recross the Mississippi, to settle down in peace, and plant their corn, and warning them if they refused that his troops would sweep over them like fire over the prairies, Black Hawk sent word that their hearts were bad, that they would not return, that Gen. Atkinson would find the grass green and not easily burnt, and that they would fight, if he sent his warriors among them. Black Hawk's force was estimated at about five hundred, subsequently increased by Winnebago and other Indians to about eight hundred warriors.

Meanwhile, Gen. Atkinson, on the 25th of April, had directed Colonel Dodge, as commanding the militia of Iowa County, Michigan Territory, to raise as many mounted men as could be obtained in that County. The first company was mustered into service on the 2d day of May, William Schuyler Hamilton, Captain, who had been with Henry Dodge in the Winnebago disturbance of 1827. While other companies were being organized, the following letter was sent to the Governor of Illinois, who was then at Dixon's Ferry with a thousand volunteers from that State:

MINERAL POINT, May 8, 1832.

His Excellency John Reynolds:

DEAR SIR.—The exposed situation of the settlements of the mining district to the attack of the Indian enemy makes it a matter of deep and vital interest to us that we should be apprised of the movements of the mounted men under your Excellency's immediate command. Black Hawk and his band, it is stated by the last advices we have had on this subject, was to locate himself about twenty miles above Dixon's Ferry, on Rock river. Should the mounted men under your command make an attack on that party, we would be in great danger here; for should you defeat Black Hawk, the retreat would be on our settlements. There are now collected within twenty miles above our settlements about two hundred Winnebagoes, and should the Sauks be forced into the Winnebago country, many of the wavering of that nation would unite with the

---

1 George Cubbage taught school at Dubuque in the winter of 1833-4; was door-keeper at the first session of the First Legislative Assembly of Wisconsin Ter., at Belmont, and Adjutant General of the Ter.; one of the Commissioners "for laying off the towns of Fort Madison, Burlington, Belleview, Dubuque, etc.," under acts of Congress, July 2d, 1836, March 3d, 1837; and an early settler in Jackson County, Iowa.

hostile Sauks. I have no doubt it is part of the policy of this banditti to unite themselves as well with the Pottawattamies as Winnebagoes. It is absolutely important to the safety of this country that the people here should be apprised of the intended movements of your army. Could you detach a part of your command across the Rock river, you would afford our settlements immediate protection, and we would promptly unite with you, with such a mounted force as we could bring into the field. Judge Gentry, Colonel Moore and James P. Cox, Esq., will wait on your Excellency and receive your orders.

I am, sir, with respect and esteem, your obedient servant.   H. DODGE,
Commanding Michigan Militia.

The Illinois troops were not in a situation to act upon the suggestion of Col. Dodge. They were soon demoralized by Stillman's defeat, May 14th, upon which Governor Reynolds the same night made a call for two thousand men, and sent an express to inform Col. Dodge of the disaster, and of the imminent danger to which the mining settlements were exposed. Meanwhile, Col. Dodge had gone himself on a scouting expedition, with a party of twenty-seven men, including his sons, Henry L., and Augustus C., to learn the movements of the enemy, and had approached near to the scene of the disaster, of which he was apprised the day following. Hastening back to the mining settlements, he hurried forward the organization of mounted companies, and the erection of stockade forts for home protection against skulking bands of savages. Eight additional companies were mustered into service before the 20th day of May. Many of the volunteers furnished their own horses. In other cases the horses were purchased or impressed. The people of nearly all the settlements, in the language of the time, "forted." Fort Union, at his home, was Col. Dodge's headquarters. His wife, when advised to repair to Galena for safety, refused, saying, "My husband and sons are between me and the Indians; I am safe so long as they live." No Spartan mother displayed greater courage. She could read her Bible and say her prayers and lie down and sleep until morning, though her youthful daughters could sleep, only to dream of Indians, and of their mother being scalped and murdered by the savages. Speaking from his own recollections fifty-one years afterwards, A. C. Dodge said: "Fathers were frequently called to defend their own thresholds, and mothers and sisters moulded bullets, and carried water, filling barrels in order to have a supply during the anticipated siege. My mother and sisters have done both. The cows were milked, and God was worshiped under the surveillance of armed men!"[1] Fort Defiance was at the farm of D. M. Parkinson, five miles southeast of Mineral Point; Fort Hamilton, at Hamilton's Lead Diggings, now Wiota; Mound Fort, at the Blue Mounds.

To keep the neighboring Winnebagoes from joining Black Hawk was a matter of first concern. For this purpose Col. Dodge and his familiar and trusted friend, Henry Gratiot, the sub-agent of the Winnebagoes, with fifty mounted volunteers from Iowa County, commanded by Captains James H. Gentry and John H. Rountree, proceeded to one of their principal villages, near the headquarters of the Four Lakes, seven miles northwest of the present capital of Wisconsin, and held a Talk with them on the 25th of May. Col. Dodge said:

My Friends.—Mr. Gratiot, your father, and myself have met to have a talk with you.

Having identified us both as your friends in making a sale of your country to the United States,[2] you will not suspect us for deceiving you.

The Sacs have shed the blood of our people. The Winnebago Prophet and, as we are told, one hundred of your people have united with Black Hawk and his party. Our people are anxious to know in what relation you stand to us, whether as friends or enemies.

Your residence being near our settlements, it is necessary and proper that we should explicitly understand from you the chiefs and warriors whether or not you intend to aid, harbor or conceal the Sacs in your country. To do so will be considered as a declaration of war on your part.

Your great American Father is the friend of the Red Skins. He wishes to make you happy. Your chiefs who have visited Washington know him well. He is mild in peace, but terrible in war. He will ask of no people what is not right, and he will submit to nothing wrong. His power is great; he commands all the warriors of the American people. If you strike us you strike him; and to make war on us, you will have your country taken from you, your annuity

1 Semi-Centennial of Iowa, p. 72.

2 H. Dodge and H. Gratiot were present at the treaty, Aug. 1, 1829, by which the Winnebago Nation agreed to relinquish the mining country lying between the Rock and Wisconsin rivers to the U. S.

money will be forfeited, and the lives of your people must be lost. We speak the words of the truth. We hope they will sink deep in your hearts.

The Sacs have killed eleven of our people, and wounded three. Our people have killed eleven of the Sacs; it was but a small detachment of our army engaged with the Sacs; when the main body of our army appeared, the Sacs ran. The Sacs have given you bad counsel. They tell you lies, and no truth. Stop your ears to their words. They know death and destruction follows them. They want you to unite with them, wishing to place you in the same situation with themselves.

We have told you the consequences of uniting with our enemies. We hope, however, the bright chain of friendship will still continue, that we may travel the same road in friendship under a clear sky. We have always been your friends. We have said you would be honest and true to your treaties. Do not let your actions deceive us. So long as you are true and faithful, we will extend the hand of friendship to you and your children; if unfaithful, you must expect to share the fate of the Sacs.

The Winnebago chiefs gave assurances of friendship and fidelity, and promised to remain at peace. Col. Dodge returned to his headquarters. A few days afterward, May 30th, learning by an express from Gen. Atkinson that Rachel and Sylvia Hall had been carried into captivity from near Ottawa, Illinois, on the 21st of May, when their parents were scalped, he took prompt measures to procure their release. A band of Winnebagoes under White Crow were stimulated by the offer of two thousand dollars made by Gen. Atkinson, to go after them. They found them in a Sac camp, and obtained their release, and brought them to the Fort at Blue Mound on the 3d of June. The same day, half-an-hour after their arrival, Col. Dodge, who had been warned of an apprehended Indian attack, came upon the ground with a mounted force. He gave White Crow and his band warm greetings, and procured for them a large beef steer, of which they made a feast. He prepared comfortable quarters for them at night in miners' cabins, and congratulated himself upon the good disposition they seemed to manifest, while not free from suspicion of their duplicity. In the course of the night he was awakened by J. P. Bion Gratiot, brother of Henry Gratiot, who rushed into his cabin, and bade him rouse up and prepare for action. He said that the Indians had left the quarters given them, had

gone into the brush, that White Crow was stirring them up to
hostility, speaking in insulting terms of Col. Dodge as "no
great shakes of a fighter," saying that Black Hawk would
make mince meat of him, as he had of Major Stillman, that
the whites could not fight, that they were a soft-shelled breed,
that they would not stand before the yell of the Red man, but
would run upon the approach of danger, and stick their heads
in the brush like turkeys or quails, that when the spear was
applied to them they would squawk like ducks; and he imita-
ted in Indian style the spearing and scalping at Stillman's
defeat, and said that all the whites who marched against the
Indians would be served the same way. White Crow told
Gratiot that he was friendly to him, and advised him to quit
Col. Dodge, and go home, and stay there. Furthermore,
said Gratiot, the Indians have been grinding their knives,
tomahawks and spears.

Col. Dodge heard these reports without saying a word;
but no one, says an eye-witness,[1] could mistake the raging
storm within his breast. He jumped to his feet, as his
informant ended, and, although ordinarily cool and collected,
he indulged upon the occasion in some severity and invective.
"Do not be alarmed," he said;" I will see that no harm befalls
you; in case of an attack, I will stand by you until the last
drop of blood is spilt. I will show the White Crow that we
are not of the soft-shelled breed, that we can stand the spear
without sqawking, that we will not run and stick our heads
in the bush." He then called the officer of the guard and his
interpreter, and, taking with them six of the guard, went to
where the Indians were, and took White Crow and five others
of his band into custody, marched them to a cabin, and
ordered them to lie down and remain there until morning; he
himself laid down by them, having first placed a strong guard
around the cabin, and a double guard around the whole
encampment. The next day the whole band, despite the com-
plaint that their feet were sore from their long travel in bring-

ing in the Hall girls, were marched to Morrison's Grove, fifteen miles west of the Blue Mounds, where Col. Dodge held a "Talk" with them in the presence of the agent, June 5th, and told them of his apprehensions that they were in sympathy with Black Hawk, as many of their young men were in his ranks, and that he must hold them as enemies, unless they gave positive assurance that they would remain neutral. White Crow answered that, although a few of their young men whose warlike temper could not be controlled were with Black Hawk, the Winnebagoes generally were friendly to the whites. Col. Dodge determined to be on the safe side, and stipulated to hold three of the Winnebagoes, Whirling Thunder, Spotted Arm, and Little Priest, as hostages for the good faith of the nation, and they were retained in the fort at Gratiot's Grove until the end of the month. It is the testimony of those who were upon the ground that this action averted an attack of the whole force of Winnebagoes who were waiting near the Four Lakes, if a favorable opportunity offered, to make a strike for Black Hawk; "but the timely movement of Col. Dodge foiled them." The Hall sisters were sent by way of Galena and St. Louis to their friends.

On the 6th of June a mounted company from Galena, commanded by Capt. J. W. Stephenson, joined Col. Dodge's forces at Gratiot's Grove. The isolation of the mining district from the rest of the country threw the people of that district upon themselves for protection, and made concerted action on the part of those in the State of Illinois and of those in Michigan Territory a necessity. There were some differences as to proper means for defence, and some jealousies arose, but a feeling of confidence in the leadership of Col. Dodge obtained throughout the region. While at Gratiot's Grove, he prepared the following address to the Volunteers now numbering about 200 mounted men, which he delivered to them the next day, upon the march to Rock River, at Kirker's Place, where they camped, on the old "Sucker trail," that ran along a branch of Apple River, in what is now Rush Township, Jo Davies County, Illinois:

VOLUNTEERS:—We have met to take the field. The tomahawk and scalping knife are drawn over the heads of the weak and defenceless inhabitants of our country. Although the most exposed people in the United States and Territories, living as we do, surrounded by savages, not a drop of the blood of the people of this part of the Territory of Michigan has been shed.[1] Let us unite, my brethren in arms. Let harmony, union, and concert exist; be vigilant, silent and cool. Discipline and obedience to orders will make small bodies of men formidable and invincible; without order and subordination, the largest bodies of armed men are no better than armed mobs. We have everything dear to freemen at stake, the protection of our frontiers, and the lives of our people. Although we have entire confidence in the Government of our choice, knowing that ours is a Government of the people, where the equal rights of all are protected, and that the power of our countrymen can crush this savage foe, yet it will take time for the Government to direct a force sufficient to give security and peace to the frontier people.

I have, Gentlemen, as well as yourselves, entire confidence both in the President of the United States and the present distinguished individual[2] at the head of the War Department; our Indian relations are better understood by them than by any two citizens who could be selected to fill their stations. They have often met our savage enemies on the field of battle where they have conquered them, as well as in council. They understand the artifice, cunning and stratagem for which our enemies are distinguished. They know our wants, and will apply the remedy. In General Atkinson, in whose protection this frontier is placed, I have entire confidence. You will recollect the responsibility he assumed for the people of this country in 1827, by ascending the Wisconsin with six hundred infantry and one hundred and fifty mounted men, to demand the murderers of our people. Many of us had the honor of serving under him on that occasion. He has my entire confidence both as a man of talents in his profession, a soldier and a gentleman. If our Government will let him retain the command, he will give us a lasting peace that will insure us tranquillity for years. He knows the resources as well as the character of the Indians we have to contend with; let the Government furnish him the means, and our troubles will be of short duration.

What, my fellow soldiers, is the character of the foe we have to contend with? They are a faithless banditti of savages who have violated all treaties. They have left the country and the nation of which they form a part. The policy of these marauders and robbers of our people appears to be, to enlist the disaffected and restless of other nations, which will give them strength and resources to murder our people and burn their property. They are the enemies of all people, both the whites and Indians. Their thirst of blood is not to be satisfied. They are willing to bring ruin and destruction on other Indians, in order to glut their vengeance on us. The humane policy of

---

1 The same day Col. Dodge was preparing this address, James Aubrey was killed by a skulking band of Indians, at the Blue Mounds, June 6th. Smith's His. of Wis., III. 209.

2 Lewis Cass.

the Government will not apply to these deluded people. Like the pirates of the sea, their hand is against every man; and the hand of every man should be against them. The future growth and prosperity of our country is to be decided for years by the policy that is now to be pursued by the Government in relation to the Indians.

Our existence as a people is at stake; and gentlemen, great as the resources of our Government are, the security of the lives of our people depends upon our vigilance, caution and bravery. The assistance of our Government may be too late for us. Let us not await the arrival of our enemies at our doors, but advance upon them, fight them, watch them, and hold them in check. Let us avoid surprise and ambuscades. Let every volunteer lie with his arms in his hands, ready for action, so that when each arises to his feet the line of battle will be formed. If attacked in the night, we will charge the enemy at a quick pace and even front. The eyes of the people are upon us; let us endeavor by our actions to retain the confidence and support of our countrymen.

Col. Dodge with his command proceeded on his march, passing over the ground of several recent Indian murders, near the present town of Polo, Illinois. They buried the dead, so far as their remains could be found; among others, those of Felix St. Vrain.[1] At this point Capt. Stephenson with his men returned to Galena. The next evening they encamped at Hickory Point, where five of their horses were stolen that night by the Indians. After reaching the camp of the U. S. regular troops at Dixon's Ferry, where Gen. Hugh Brady, who had just come from Detroit, was in command, Col. Dodge with twenty-five men escorted Gen. Brady to the rapids of the Illinois River (now Ottawa), where Gen. Atkinson was receiving new levies of Illinois volunteers. Here plans of the

---

1 Mr. St. Vrain was the trustworthy and meritorious U. S. Agent for the confederate tribe of Sacs and Foxes, including Black Hawk's band. He was distinguished for intelligence, integrity, and for the deep interest he had manifested in the welfare of all the Indians confided to his charge. He spoke their language, and they, according to their custom, had formally adopted him not only as a friend, but a brother. Notwithstanding all this, when the parties confronted each other on the 22d of May, St. Vrain, in the act of extending the hand of friendship, and addressing words of imploration to the Chief "Little Bear," not to spare his life, but to desist from war against the whites, was shot down with his associates by those whom he had fed and sheltered, and with whom he was as intimate as a brother. The bodies of himself and companions were mangled in the most shocking manner. Mr. St. Vrain was a brother-in-law of ex-Senator George W Jones, of this State. A. C. Dodge. Semi-Centennial of Iowa, p. 73.

campaign were considered. It being impossible for the U. S.
Commissary to supply Col. Dodge's command with subsistence and forage, Gen. Atkinson directed Col. Dodge, by
letter of June 11th, 1832, to procure them. Having received
his orders, Col. Dodge returned to Dixon's Ferry, reaching
there about midnight, and early the following morning, June
13th, put his command in motion for Gratiot's Grove, where,
after two days march they arrived worn and fatigued. For
eight days they had been constantly on the march; the horses
with no subsistence but grass. The men were remanded to
their respective forts for a few days, to recruit their horses.
Col. Dodge delivered a "Talk" from Gen. Atkinson to the
Winnebago hostages, and sent them with a confidential man,
Emile,[1] a French trader, on an expedition to ascertain, if possible, where the Sacs were encamped. He addressed the
following letter to a merchant at Galena with reference to
supplies for his troops, and for families in the mining district
who had been driven from their homes, and who were now
destitute and unable to provide for themselves in the suspen-
sion of all labor and business:

GRATIOT'S GROVE, June 14th, 1832.

DEAR SIR:—I was at the headquarters of Gen. Atkinson, at the mouth of
the Fox River of the Illinois, on the 11th inst. He is actively engaged in making preparations to march against the hostile Indians. He will bring into the
field about 3,000 men. I will copy for your information that part of my order
as respects the supplies of provisions for the use of the troops under my command: "Your detached situation renders it impossible for me to furnish subsistence for your troops; you will therefore procure supplies upon the best
terms practicable, and in the issue not exceed the U. S. allowance, and at the
same time be careful to have the accounts kept accurately."

I have copied that part of Gen. Atkinson's order in which you are interested.

Although it would seem from his order that the rations furnished those not
under arms would not be paid for, the Government of the United States will
certainly pay for rations furnished the inhabitants, the protection of whose

---

[1] Mentioned in the Treaty with the Winnebagoes, at Prairie du Chien,
August 1st, 1829, as "Oliver Amelle;" U. S. Statutes at Large, VII, 324;
written "Emmell," by Col. Dodge in his letter of July 14th, 1833, to Gen.
Atkinson; he built the first house, a trading house, where is now the Capital
of Wisconsin. Wis. His. Coll., X. 69.

lives makes it necessary for them to *fort* themselves, to avoid the tomahawk and scalping knife. The people of the country have been invited here by the agents of the Government to settle in this country, to work the lead mines. They are neither intruders nor squatters on the public lands. The Government has by the industry and enterprise of the people of the mining country derived all the advantages which they could have anticipated in the working and exploration of their mines. The Government has no regular troops here to afford protection to our exposed settlements, and I have no hesitation in saying that the rations furnished women and children will be paid for by a special appropriation to be made by Congress.

The only difference with you, as I confidently believe, will be that the amount due you for furnishing the troops under my immediate command will be paid for promptly by the War Department, and for the residue a special law will have to be passed.

This is a subject of great importance to the inhabitants who have been driven from their homes by the savages. Unless they can be furnished on the credit of the Government, starvation must ensue, as many of them are unable to leave this country, and they are also unable to furnish themselves. I will thank you to write me on this subject as early as possible.

I am, with much respect, your obedient servant,

H. DODGE,

Col. Commanding the Militia of Iowa County, M. T.

MR. JOHN ATCHISON, Galena.

The same day he proceeded to his home at Fort Union. Murderous bands were infesting the country. Ere he entered his house he was informed of the killing of Aubrey at the Blue Mounds. Fear and terror prevailed. At midnight word came that seven men had been surprised that day six miles southeast of Ft. Hamilton, on the Pecatonica, while at work in a corn-field, of whom five were killed, and two had escaped. He despatched an express to Capt. Gentry at the Platte Mounds, to march to the place and bury the dead, and find out the number and movements of the enemy. The news reached Ft. Defiance earlier, and Lt. Bracken with ten men marched from that post the same night to Ft. Hamilton, and the next day collected the remains of the dead, and buried them. At a council that evening, Capt. Gentry and his men having arrived, it was agreed that if Col. Dodge did not arrive by 8 o'clock next morning, those present would take the trail, and pursue the Indians. Meanwhile, Col. Dodge had first gone to the Blue Mounds to leave orders and see the situation there, and had then scoured the country to within ten miles of Ft. Hamilton, where he camped for the night at Fretwell's Diggings.

The next morning, June 16th, about a mile from the Fort, Col. Dodge left the main road, which passed round a field, and took a by-path, to shorten the distance. Coming into the main road again he met a German (Henry Apple) on a good horse, which Capt. Gentry had wanted to impress into the service; but Apple said that if he might go to his cabin for his blankets he would join the expedition. After a few inquiries Col. Dodge passed on, and Apple went along upon the main road. At the time eleven Indians were lying on that road in ambush, within 150 yards. Before reaching the Fort, Col. Dodge heard three guns fired, and at first supposed it was Capt. Gentry's men shooting at a target. In an instant Apple's horse came galloping back, without rider, the saddle bloody, a bullet-hole through the top of his neck and ear.

It afterward appeared that the Indians had first waylaid the by-path, but at this time had moved over to the main road. Had Col. Dodge kept that road, or had he arrived half an hour earlier upon the by-path, he would have fallen into the ambuscade, instead of Apple.

At the Fort all was wild excitement. Many were for rushing pell-mell after the Indians. Instantly Col. Dodge with stentorian voice ordered the men to "saddle up." He said: "Fellow-soldiers—We shall immediately follow the Indians, and overtake them if possible. We know not their number. If any of you cannot charge them sword in hand, fall back now, as I want none with me but those on whom I can rely in any emergency." None fell back. Twenty-nine mounted men joined Col. Dodge in the pursuit. They passed the scalped and mangled body of Apple, butchered in a shocking manner. Says Col. Dodge in his report to Gen. Atkinson, written two days afterward from Ft. Union

The Indians had not more than thirty minutes start. They retreated through a thicket of undergrowth, almost impassable for horsemen; they scattered to prevent our trailing them. **Finding we had** open prairie around the thicket, I despatched **part of** my men to look **for** the trail **of the Indians in** the open ground. In running our horses about two miles, **we saw** them about half a mile **ahead,** trotting along at their ease; they were making for the low ground, where it **would** be difficult for us to pursue them on horseback. **Two** of the small streams had such steep banks as to oblige us to dismount, and jump our horses down the banks, and force our way over the best way we **could.** **This delay** again gave the Indians the start, but my horses being good, **and men eager in the** pursuit, I gained on them rapidly. They were directing **their course to a** bend of the Pecatonica, covered with a deep swamp, which they reached before I could cross that stream, owing to the steepness **of** the banks, and the **depth** of the water. After crossing the Pecatonica, in **the** open ground I dismounted my command, linked my horses, left four **men in** charge of them, and **sent** four men in different directions to watch **the movements of the** Indians, if they should **attempt to** swim the Pecatonica; **the men were placed on** high points that would **give** a view of the enemy, **should they attempt to** retreat. I formed my men on **foot at** open order, and at **trailed arms, and we** proceeded through the swamps **to some** timber and undergrowth, where **I expected to** find the enemy When I found their trail, I knew they were **close at hand; they** had got close **to the** edge of the lake, where the bank was **about six feet high,** which **was a** complete breastwork for them. They commenced **the fire,** when three of my men fell, two dangerously wounded, one severely **but not dangerously.** I instantly ordered a charge **on them** made by eighteen men, **which was promptly obeyed. The Indians** being under the bank, our guns **were brought within** ten or fifteen **feet of them** before we **could fire** on them. Their party consisted of thirteen men. **Eleven were** killed **on** the spot, and the remaining two were killed **in crossing the lake, so that they** were left without one to **carry the** news **to their friends.**

The volunteers under my **command behaved** with **great gallantry.** It would be impossible **for** me to discriminate **among** them; **at the word** "charge," the men rushed forward, and literally **shot** the Indians **to pieces.** We were, Indians **and** whites, **on a piece of** ground not to exceed **sixty** feet square.

A part of the scalps were **given to** the Sioux and Menomonies **as well as the Winnebagoes.** Col. Hamilton had arrived with these Indians **about one hour after our defeating** the hostile Sacs. The friendly Indians appeared **delighted with** the scalps. **They** went to the ground where the Indians **were killed, and cut** them literally **to pieces.**

The Indian commander was a big, **burly** brave, often **running back** during the charge to encourage his men, **and haranguing** them in battle. **In the thick** of the **fight** he came toward Col. Dodge with **his** gun on his shoulder, halted at a few **paces, drew** the trigger, and was disappointed in his gun not going **off.** The same instant Col. **Dodge** brought his **rifle** in position, pulled the trigger, but **from** dampness of **the pow-**

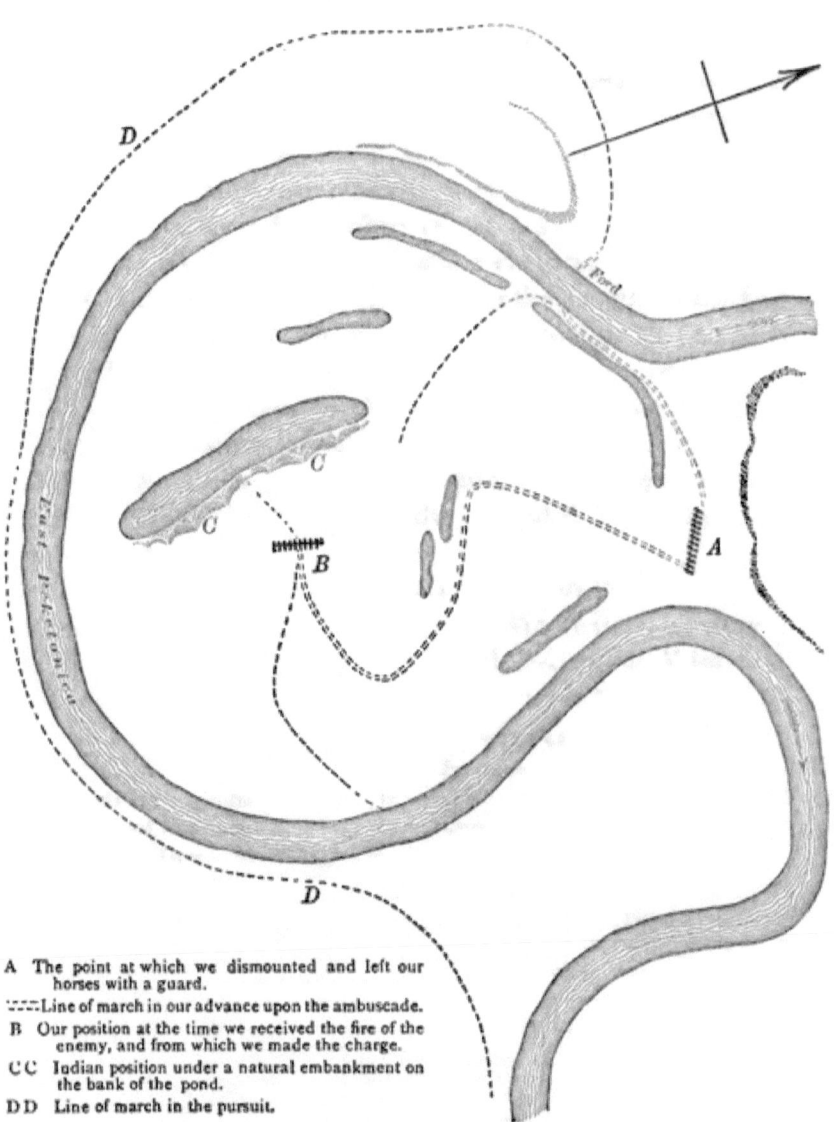

A The point at which we dismounted and left our
   horses with a guard.
⋯⋯Line of march in our advance upon the ambuscade.
B Our position at the time we received the fire of the
   enemy, and from which we made the charge.
C C Indian position under a natural embankment on
   the bank of the pond.
D D Line of march in the pursuit.

BATTLE OF HORSE SHOE BEND, JUNE 16, 1832.

der it did not go off. Meantime the brave approached, knife in hand; when only a few feet away, Col. Dodge shot him down with his pistol.

The scene of the battle, Horse Shoe Bend, was about two miles and a half from Fort Hamilton, on section eleven in what is now Wiota township. After various discomfitures on the part of different bodies of troops that had taken the field, this was the first victory over the hostile Sacs. "It was considered the most brilliant affair of the war, and was entirely in keeping with the General's former character," says an officer of the regular army,[1] who received the details of the affair from an eye-witness a few days subsequently. "This little action," said Governor Ford,"[2] will equal any for courage, brilliancy and success in the whole history of Indian wars." It brought a sense of relief to the mining settlements, and revived confidence along the frontier. The troops returned to Fort Hamilton, conveying the wounded partly by litter, partly by wagon.

The next morning a "talk" was had with the friendly Indians. The following extracts from MS. letters, preserved in the Library of the State Historical Society of Wisconsin, explain the appearance of these Indians upon the scene:

J. M. STREET TO T. P. BURNETT.

PRAIRIE DU CHIEN, Feb. 1, 1832.

The Menomonees and Sioux are preparing for a retaliatory war this spring.[3] The Sacs and Foxes, I learn, expect retaliation, and will be in preparation to meet them. Therefore a bloody contest may be expected.

GEN. ATKINSON TO J. M. STREET.

HEADQUARTERS RIGHT WING WESTERN DEPARTMENT, }
DIXON'S FERRY, ROCK RIVER, May 26, 1832. }

I have to request that you will send to me at this place with as little delay

---

1 E. Buckner, in Michigan Pioneer Coll., xii, 424–436.

2 His. of Illinois, p. 128.

3 A party of twenty-eight Menomonees had been stolen upon and murdered by a band of Sacs and Foxes near Prairie du Chien a few months before. It was for the purpose of demanding the surrender of the murderers, and in the interest of peace between those tribes, that Gen. Atkinson was on his way up the Mississippi from Jefferson Barracks at the very time Black Hawk crossed over into Illinois.

as possible as many Menomonee **and** Sioux Indians as can be collected within a striking distance **of** Prairie **du Chien.** I **want to** employ them in conjunction with the troops against **the Sac and Fox Indians,** who are now some 40 or 50 miles above **us in** a state **of war against the** whites. I understand the Menomonees to the number **of 300** warriors, who were a few days ago with you, are anxious to **take** part with **us.** Do encourage them to do so, and **promise them** rations, blankets, pay, etc. I have written Capt. **Loomis to** furnish **them** some arms, if they can be spared, and ammunition.

Col. Hamilton, who has volunteered his services to lead **the Indians to this place,** will hand you this **letter,** and, **if** the Menomonees and Sioux can be **prevailed upon to** come, **will** perform **the duty.** I have to desire that Mr. **Marsh may be** sent with **Col.** H. and **the Indians,** and an interpreter of the **Menomonee** language.

J. M. STREET TO T. P. BURNETT.

PRAIRIE DU CHIEN, May 30, 1832.

You will proceed with John Marsh to the nearest **Sioux villages, and** render him such aid as **may** be necessary in obtaining as many **of the Indians as** you may be enabled, to come **down** with you, and **proceed** under the command of Mr. Marsh to join **Gen. Atkinson.** Use every means of persuasion to expedite the object, and hasten **your return, as** much depends on expedition.

T. P. BURNETT TO J. M. STREET.

PRAIRIE DU CHIEN, June 5, 1832.

In obedience to your order I set out immediately from this place in company with **Mr. Marsh in a canoe, and eight hands, to** visit the **nearest** village of the Sioux **Indians.**

From **recent indications among the Winnebagoes of the** Upper Mississippi of a **disposition to engage in hostilities against the Sacs** and Foxes, Mr. Marsh **and myself** concluded to call **at their village upon the river of** Prairie **a la** Crosse, **and** invite as many **of them as should choose to do so,** to join us **upon** our return. We arrived at the **Winnebago** village on **the** evening of **the next day** after **our** departure, **and on that** night had a talk with the chiefs and **braves** upon the **subject.** Winoashikan was opposed to the measure, **and did not want to have anything** to do with the business. He **said** that **the Sacs had this season twice** presented the red wampum to the Winnebagoes **at the Portage, and that they as often** washed it white, and handed **it back to them, that he did not like that red thing,** he was afraid of it. Wandykhatakan took up **the wampum, and said that he** with all the young **men of the** village would **go, that they were anxious to** engage **in** the **expedition,** and would be ready **to accompany us upon our** return.

The **next day we** arrived at Prairie **aux** Ailes, and found the **Sioux** extremely anxious **to go** against the Sacs **and** Foxes. They were intending to make a descent against them in a few days, **if** they had **not** been **sent** for. Although they engaged **in** their preparations with great **alacrity, we** found it necessary **to wait** until Monday morning to give them time **to** have everything **ready** for **the expedition.**

We set out on our return at 9 A. M., accompanied by the whole effective force of the band, and at Prairie a la Crosse were joined by about twenty warriors of the Winnebagoes, who told us that the remainder of their village would follow the next day. We reached this place to-day with about 100 warriors. I think from the disposition manifested by the Winnebagoes their number will be augmented to fifty or sixty, before the expedition leaves Prairie du Chien, making a force of Sioux and Winnebagoes of 130 or 140 warriors. The Indians appear well affected toward the whites, are in high spirits and seem anxious for an opportunity to engage the Sacs and Foxes.

I made the Indians the promises authorized by Gen. Atkinson's letter for subsistence, pay, etc., and told them that their families would be supplied with provisions during their absence from home. The most of the families of the warriors have accompanied them thus far, to take a supply of provisions home with them, when the expedition shall have left this place. Mr. Marsh has displayed great zeal and energy in effecting the object of our visit, and his exertions had a happy effect in bringing out the greatest possible force from the Bands called upon.

The Indian allies, however, proved to be of no service, but betrayed a cowardly spirit. Some of them said that they were willing to fight the Sacs, but they wanted to return first, and make better preparation. They consumed an enormous quantity of beef, and there was a scarcity of subsistence. It was deemed best on the whole to send them back up the Mississippi. In his report to Gen. Atkinson, quoted above, Col. Dodge added:

I was extremely anxious to retain them. They would have acted as spies, and would have kept the enemy in a state of check, while we were recruiting our horses for the expedition. Whether the Indians will return or not, I am at a loss to say. The Winnebagoes make solemn promises; I hope they will not deceive us. We are doing everything in our power to conciliate them. Decorra says that the whole of the Rock River Indians (Winnebagoes) are over the Wisconsin; that they have left the Sacs entire possession of the country; that they (the Sacs) are now high up the Rock river, where there is but little for them to live on, and they must perish for want. This I can not believe. I have been told there is fish in great abundance, upon which alone they can no doubt subsist.

From his home at Ft. Union he was called to Galena, to look after the supplies for destitute families, for which he had to make himself personally responsible. At Galena he was honored with the presentation of a flag from the ladies, with the sentiment, "The Daughters of the Lead-Mines to our Father War-Chief." Soon afterwards, a double-barrelled gun was forwarded to him by citizens of Prairie du Chien, in testimony of their respect for his valor, with the following letter:

PRAIRIE DU CHIEN, 2d July, 1832.

Dear General:—I had hoped upon my return from Kentucky and the East to have had the pleasure of seeing you before this time, but, as that has been denied me, I have been much gratified to hear of the patriotic efforts which you have been making for the defence of our common country. Your sacrifices, zeal, energy, and success in defending our exposed frontier, almost without means, will not be forgotten by the Government, and will live in the grateful recollections of your fellow-citizens.

The people of this place have not viewed without deep interest the scene. Although they have not done much to aid in the defence of their more exposed countrymen, they have looked with intense anxiety to the result of every movement, and numbers would have left their homes, had it been thought consistent with the safety of this place, and attached themselves to your standard. But you know the character of the mass of our population, and the little that is to be expected from them in offensive operations. And even in defence, they are not likely to act efficiently or in concert until a few shall be killed by the enemy. Besides, they have been in a state of almost constant alarm since my return, for fear of an attack upon this place, which has forbidden all idea of volunteering for the defence of any other part of the country.

I had it in contemplation, although crippled in one of my thighs, and not having perfect health for eight months, to return with Capt. Estes, and offer my feeble aid in effecting the punishment which those ruthless savages deserve. But I was informed two days since, that the first mail from below would most likely bring me an order for my removal to St. Peters. The agent has left that place on furlough, and the sub-agent has resigned, leaving no one to manage the business of the Department. I am therefore holding myself in readiness for a change of location. I am not vain enough, however, to suppose that this can be of any material consequence to you or the country, and I trust that the time is not far distant when the services of none of our citizens will be required in the field, and all who survive the conflict will be enabled to return to their families and homes.

I am pleased to learn that there is now a sufficient force in the field to act decisively against the hostile savages, and I hope that no terms will be made with them until they are punished in so signal a manner as to quell forever their disposition to war against our country. You and the brave men under your command have given an earnest of what you will do when you shall be properly supported, and I doubt not when the day of meeting shall come that you will give a good account of those who shall come to your hands.

I regret that the Indians collected here and forwarded to the army have proven so useless. The Siouxs, I believe, are cowards, and the feelings of the Winnebagoes are as much against us as for us, probably more so; yet their interest and their fears will keep them at least neutral. I have no apprehension that they will act as a body against us, unless our army should be defeated, which must be out of the range of all probability. The Menominees would be serviceable, if there were enough of them. They are a brave, docile and faithful people, but the number which could be raised this side of Green Bay is too small to be of much importance.

I from the first doubted the expediency of calling in the aid of the friendly tribes, and so expressed myself before I left this place to collect the Indians, though in obedience to orders I set out with Mr. Marsh at a minute's warning to assemble and bring them to this place, and I have no hesitation in saying that we performed the duty as promptly as it could have been done. I have always considered Indians, to be the most troublesome and expensive of all allies, at the same time that their services can be least relied upon. The result of this expedition is an additional evidence to support the opinion.

I hope the next Express will bring us the intelligence of some brilliant achievement decisive of the controversy. Could you gain so much time, it would give me great pleasure to hear from you, but I know the incessant fatigue you must undergo, and the constant employment of your time required by your active exertions. Whenever you can, please write me, and believe me, most truly,　　　　　　Your friend and obedient servant,

　　　　　　　　　　　　　　　　　　　T. P. BURNETT.

　　　　　　　　　　　PRAIRIE DU CHIEN, 3d July, 1832.

Gen. Henry Dodge, Fort Union:

The undersigned citizens of Prairie du Chien have witnessed with feelings of high respect and admiration the patriotic exertions which you have made for the defense of our frontier against the cruelties of savage warfare. Fully appreciating the bold and energetic course you have pursued, we send by the hands of Capt. James B. Estes a double-barrelled gun, which we hope you will accept as a small testimony of the high estimation in which we hold your character as an officer and a citizen.

　　　　　　　　Your obedient servants,

H. L. DOUSEMAN,	JOS. M. STREET,
M. BRISBOIS,	T. P. BURNETT,
J. BRISBOIS,	JEAN CRUNET,
M. B. W. BRISBOIS,	WM. M. REED.

Upon returning from Galena, Col. Dodge made an expedition the 24th of June to the Blue Mounds, where two men had recently fallen into an ambush. Edward B. Beouchard related this incident of himself:

On the 4th of June, when Capt. James Aubrey was killed, I started to get his body, and asked Lt. Force to go with me; but he refused, and I told him if he got killed, and was only six feet off, I would not go for his body. When Force and Green were killed on the 20th, and I went and got Green's remains, and brought them to the Fort, they asked me if I could hold spite against a dead man. I replied that I would do what I said, whether a man was dead or alive; and Lt. Force's body laid where it fell for four days.

Col. Dodge and his troops found Lt. Force's body, which had been cruelly mutilated, and buried it. They reconnoitred the country to the head of Sugar river, but discovered no Sacs.

On the 28th of June the whole army of Gen. Atkinson was set in pursuit of Black Hawk. It consisted of 400 regular infantry and about 2600 mounted volunteers; many of the volunteers had been disabled by sickness and exposure. The army moved up the Rock river country in three divisions: Gen. Atkinson with Gen. Henry's brigade formed the right wing; Gen. Alexander's command formed the center, Gen. Posey's brigade, with Col. Dodge's battalion, formed the left wing. They were to meet at Lake Koshkonong.

Col. Dodge rendezvoused his forces, in all about 200 men, at Fort Hamilton, where he was joined by Posey's brigade. Gen. Atkinson had tendered the command of this brigade to Col. Dodge; but Col. Dodge declined it in an address to the brigade unless elected by the officers and men. Major John Dement, of the Spy battalion, 1st brigade Illinois volunteers, personally a stranger to Col. Dodge at the time, was earnest in advocating his election. "He will lead us to victory," he said, "and retrieve for us the honors we have lost at Stillman's Run and at Kellogg's Grove." The election resulted in Posey's favor, by one company. "In our march," says Hon. George W. Jones, who was aid to Col. Dodge, "men and officers of Posey's brigade told me that they voted against Col. Dodge, and for their old neighbor and friend, because they were assured Col Dodge would put them in the front, in places of danger; an honor I told them Col. Dodge would not deprive his command of." At this time a feeling of resentment on the part of Col. Dodge towards Capt. W. S. Hamilton for disobedience of orders with reference to the friendly Indians was aggravated: Hon. G. W. Jones says:

The day of the election, as we rode past Fort Hamilton, Col. Dodge was hailed by Capt. Hamilton The Colonel, at my thrice repeated request, stopped his horse (Big Black), and, as Hamilton approached, sprang off, and presented Hamilton with the butt ends of his two pistols, and entreated him to take choice, that the qestion might be settled there and then which was to be commander. Hamilton at once threw up both hands, and sitting down on the hill-side declined to fight. I urged the Colonel to remount, which he did, and we rode on to the encampment of Gen. Posey.[1]

Col. Dodge's battalion marched with the left wing of the army, July 1-4, by way of the Pecatonica battle-field and Sugar River Diggings near to the first of the Four Lakes, where they were joined by White Crow's band; thence through almost impassable swamps to the mouth of Whitewater, July 6th, where Black Hawk was reported to be. At this point an express from Gen. Atkinson ordered them to his camp on Bark River. Col. Dodge chafed under this order as thwarting his plans. After reaching Gen. Atkinson's encampment, the region was reconnoitred by scouts in a fruitless search for Black Hawk. Many believed that he had taken to the swamps beyond the reach of the army, and that no more danger was to be apprehended from him. Gen. Atkinson built block-houses where the village of Ft. Atkinson now stands. Governor Reynolds and a number of Illinois officers did not believe there would be any fighting, and left the field on the 9th, to return home.

The army was now short of provisions from losses in swimming rivers, by the miring of horses in creeks and swamps, and from waste by the volunteers. The regulars took better care of their rations, and were not in want. In this juncture, Gen. Atkinson ordered Alexander's and Henry's brigades and Dodge's battalion, to march to Ft. Winnebago, a distance of 40 miles, for supplies, with verbal instructions to pursue the trail of the enemy, if it was met with in going or returning. At Fort Winnebago, Col. Dodge secured the co-operation of Pierre Pauquette, a half-breed, whom he had

---

1 Hamilton was one of my father's captains both in the war of '27 and '32. Although they had some unpleasant personal difficulties, ephemeral in their nature, my brother, sisters and myself were on excellent terms with him. He was one of the most interesting and clever of Wisconsin pioneers, and in many respects a most remarkable and meritorious man.—*A C Dodge to Cyrus Woodman, July 3, 1883.*

known as an interpreter, and a dozen Winnebagoes. Getting new information as to the whereabouts of the enemy, that they had moved further up Rock River, Col. Dodge called a council of his officers with those of the other two commands, and proposed to return by a circuit in that direction.[1] Gen. Henry coincided, but Gen. Alexander advocated a return by the route they had come, as pursuant to their orders. The result was that Gen. Alexander returned directly with the supplies and the worn-down horses, while Gen. Henry and Col. Dodge diverged on their march some thirty miles to the east.

Col. Dodge's effective force was now reduced to one hundred and fifty men; Gen. Henry's to about four hundred and fifty. At the Rapids of Rock River (now Heustisford) they found a few emaciated Winnebagoes, who reported that the Sacs had moved up to Cranberry Lake (now Horicon Lake, Dodge Co.) Encamping for the night, July 18th, they set a double guard, and sent Adjutants Merriam and Wood-bridge, with Little Thunder, a Winnebago chief, as guide, to carry dispatches to Gen. Atkinson. But after going eight or ten miles the dispatch fell upon a fresh trail of the enemy bearing westward, and returned to camp with the information. It was at once determined to pursue this trail in the morning, and advices to that effect were sent to Gen. Atkinson.

Much of the pursuit was over swamps and morasses, and through tangled thickets; in the midst of which the soldiers were drenched with heavy rains. Towards evening of the second day of the pursuit, July 20, the scouts discovered a large body of Indians near the Third Lake, who fled into the adjacent woods; a band of them were stretched along Catfish Creek,

---

[1] I was there, and my father, D. M. Parkinson, was there, and commanded a Company. He was a compeer of Col. Dodge and Gen. Henry, and a warm personal friend of both, and was admitted to their councils upon this and all other occasions; so was Capt. Gentry, to whose Company I then belonged. My father informed me at the time that Col. Dodge was the suggester and prime mover in this matter, Gen. Henry assenting to and approving of the course at once.—*Peter Parkinson, Jr.*

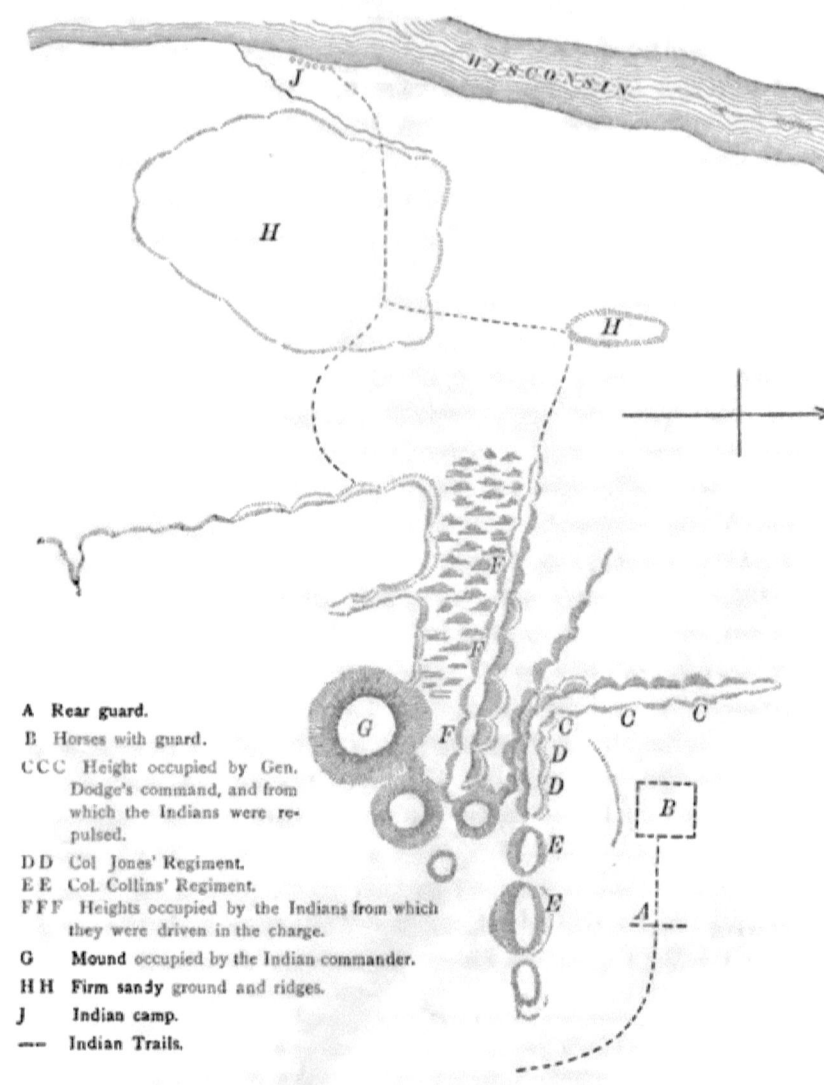

A   Rear guard.

B   Horses with guard.

C C C   Height occupied by Gen.
        Dodge's command, and from
        which the Indians were re-
        pulsed.

D D   Col Jones' Regiment.

E E   CoL Collins' Regiment.

F F F   Heights occupied by the Indians from which
        they were driven in the charge.

G   Mound occupied by the Indian commander.

H H   Firm sandy ground and ridges.

J   Indian camp.

---   Indian Trails.

BATTLE OF WISCONSIN HEIGHTS, JULY 21, 1832.

in what is now the eastern part of the city of Madison; they all decamped in the night. Pursuit was resumed early the next morning, the troops passing over the ground now occupied by the city of Madison. After a march of about thirty miles, in which the scouts kept up a running fire, the main body of the enemy were overtaken upon the bluffs of the Wisconsin, between 3 and 4 o'clock in the afternoon. Col. Dodge and Major Wm. L. D. Ewing with their commands were in the advance. They dismounted, and at the edge of the bluff were met by a rally of the enemy, attacking Capt. Dixon's spy company which was then in the front. Here the Indians were repulsed. Gen. Henry soon came up, and deployed his forces; Col. Collins' regiment taking position on the left, Col. Jones' regiment in the center, leaving Col. Dodge on the right. In this order they charged the enemy, and drove him from position to position. In the midst of a heavy rain the enemy were pursued into the river bottom, when night closed upon the scene.

In the morning it was found that the enemy had all crossed the Wisconsin River. Despatches were sent to Gen. Atkinson. Capt. Estes was dispatched to Prairie du Chien with the following letter to the commandant at Ft. Crawford, Capt. Loomis:

CAMP WISCONSIN, July 22, 1832.

We met the enemy yesterday near the Wisconsin river, and opposite the old Sac village, after a close pursuit for near one hundred miles. Our loss was one man killed and eight wounded. From the scalps taken by the Winnebagoes, as well as those taken by the whites, and the Indians carried from the field of battle, we must have killed forty of them. The number of wounded is not known; we can only judge from the number killed that many were wounded. From their crippled situation I think we must overtake them, unless they descend the Wisconsin by water If you could place a field-piece immediately on the Wisconsin that would command the river, you might prevent their escape by water.

Gen. Atkinson will arrive at the Blue Mounds on the 24th with the regulars and a brigade of mounted men. I will cross the Wisconsin to-morrow. Should the enemy retreat by land, he will probably attempt crossing some twenty miles above Prairie du Chien; in that event the mounted men would want some boats for the transportation of their arms, ammunition and provisions.

If you could procure for us some Mackinaw boats in that event, as well as some provision supplies, it would greatly facilitate our views. Excuse great haste.　　　　　　　　　　　　　　**Your** obedient servant,

H. DODGE,

Col. Commanding Michigan Mounted Volunteers.

Col. Dodge did not cross the Wisconsin on the 23d, as was originally intended, but marched to the Blue Mounds, looking after supplies, and awaiting the arrival of Gen. Atkinson. The effective force of the whole army now numbered about 1200 men. The Indians having been traced several miles down the river, the troops rendezvoused at Helena. At this point some pine log buildings were pulled down, and made into small rafts, on which slowly and with difficulty the whole army crossed the river on the 27th and 28th. On the next day they struck the trail of the Indians, and for four days they pursued them over a rough and hilly country to the Mississippi, near the Bad Axe, and came up with them on the morning of August 2d.

The order of battle was arranged under the personal supervision of Gen. Atkinson. Col. Dodge's squadron, whose scouts had been constantly in the advance, and the U. S. Infantry under Col. Zachary Taylor, were placed in the front; the Illinois brigades followed, Posey and Alexander on the right, Henry on the left. In this order the army marched down the bluff into the thickets and timber of the river bottom, plunged through a bayou, and in a few minutes met the yells of the enemy, and closed with them. No quarters were asked; none were taken prisoners but squaws and children. The troops of the different commands vied with each other in gaining positions of bravery and danger. The action continued for three hours, the Indians being driven from tree to tree and from one hiding-place to another, until they were utterly routed and dispersed, with a loss on their part of 150 killed. At the last it was more a massacre than a battle. Many were shot down in the river; others fell into the hands of their hereditary enemies, the Sioux.

Gen. Atkinson reported a loss among his troops of twenty-four killed and wounded, of whom six were in Dodge's battalion, a larger relative proportion than under any other command. In the progress of the fight positions were changed. Col. Taylor with the U. S. Infantry and Col. Dodge with his squadron in following the rear guard of the enemy were thrown upon the extreme right, while Gen. Henry gained the front with his brigade. "Both brave officers," says Wakefield, an Illinois historian, who was in the engagement, "they would have gloried in being in the front, but this was intended by the God of battles for our beloved Henry." The following order was issued the day after the battle:

HEADQUARTERS 1ST ARMY CORPS OF THE NORTHWESTERN ARMY, }
BANK OF THE MISSISSIPPI, NEAR BAD AXE RIVER, August 3, 1832. }

Order No. 65.

The victory achieved by the volunteers and regular troops over the enemy yesterday on this ground affords the Commanding General an opportunity of expressing his approbation of their brave conduct. The whole of the troops participated in the honor of the combat; some of the corps, however, were more fortunate than others in being thrown from their position in order of battle more immediately in conflict with the enemy; these were Henry's Brigade, Dodge's Battalion, the Regular Troops, Leech's Regiment of Posey's Brigade, and the Spy Battalion of Alexander's Brigade.

In order that individual merit and the conduct of the Corps may be properly represented to the Department of War and the General commanding the Northwestern Army, the Commanding General of this division directs that commanding officers of brigades and independent corps make to him written reports of the conduct and operation of their respective Commands in the action.

By order of BRIG. GENERAL ATKINSON.

ALB. S. JOHNSTON, A. D. C. and A. Adt. Gen'l.

In his jealousy for the fame of Gen. Henry, Governor Thomas Ford, in his History of Illinois, ch. V, disparaged both Gen. Atkinson and Col. Dodge. The truth is, that they all were brave men, intent upon their duty, while as intimated in the above order, the fortune of war, and their own earnest spirit as well, gave Dodge and Henry foremost positions which they sustained with honor. There was a perfect understanding and a harmony of action between those officers from the beginning. Henry was the younger. His father had fought under Dodge in the war of 1812. Appreciating his experience and prowess as an old soldier and an Indian-fighter, Henry confided in Dodge's skill and judgment, and deferred to him in council and in the field. He was immediately appointed a Captain in the U. S. Rangers under Dodge, with the rank of first Captain in that battalion, but his health failing he left the service, and went to New Orleans for a milder climate, and died in that city, March 4th, 1834. Henry County, Iowa, was named for him.

After the battle, when Gen. Atkinson met Col. Dodge at Prairie du Chien, he threw his arms around him, and said to him, "Dodge, you have saved me; you have dragged me on to victory." President Jackson had been impatient with the slowness of military movements, and had sent word to Gen. Atkinson that he must bring the war to an end or he would remove him.

Early in the battle of Bad Axe, Black Hawk and the Prophet fled, and attempted flight to Canada. After the battle, Col. Dodge called Waukon-Decorra to him, and told him that their Great Father at Washington wanted the big warriors taken. Parties were sent in search of them, and they were captured and delivered up to the Indian agent at Prairie du Chien on the 27th of August. Black Hawk said that he would have whipt the whites, and gone where he pleased in the mining country, had it not been for "Hairy Face" (Col. Dodge).

In the course of a discussion in the U. S. Senate the following winter upon the public lands, the Hon. Alexander Buckner, of Missouri, associated the name of Henry Dodge with that of George Rogers Clark among "the gallant sons of the west." He said, January 12th, 1883:

Look at the movements of the troops last summer. What common claim has any but the West to the fame of the heroic Dodge, of whom it may be said that he was born, trained, and seasoned in all the hardships, all the privations and dangers of the West, and is justly entitled to a share in all her glories.

The Hon. Samuel McRoberts, Senator from Illinois, gave a similar testimony in the Senate on the 25th of June, 1841.

That war (of 1832) came from a race of men who do not precede hostilities by wordy negotiations, make no formal declarations of the purpose, give no other notice than the war-whoop and the sound of the rifle, who seldom give quarter, and who count their victories by the number of scalps they have taken. The gallant men of the Territory came to the rescue. Gen. Dodge organized a small but intrepid corps, who took the field, and, as far as possible, staid the plague, until the volunteers from Illinois and a few companies of the army could be brought to their relief. During this period the enemy waylaid all the roads, and murdered many of the inhabitants. One incident will illustrate the character of Gen. Dodge and his followers. The enemy came to the Pecatonica, and murdered some of the citizens. Dodge and his party pursued them. The enemy, finding they could not make their escape, posted themselves for battle. Now here was a situation to test the courage and devotion of any man to his country. The enemy were armed with the rifle, tomahawk, and spear, which they had been accustomed to use all their lives. They had a decided advantage in position, and were enabled to have their usual advantage, the first fire. To dislodge them a charge must be made in the most exposed of all possible situations, and, from the number and desperation of the enemy, at a great sacrifice of human life. In such a situation what is the course of Dodge and his brave associates? They never hesitate. They resolve to dislodge the enemy, or perish in the attempt. They dismount from their horses, and, headed by their commander, charged the enemy on foot. They received the enemy's fire almost at the muzzle of their guns. A desperate conflict ensued. After each party had delivered its fire, it became a personal encounter between the combatants. The story is soon told. The enemy all fell. Not a man of them was left to tell the tale. I met Dodge and the survivors of his party a few days afterward, and some of them still carried upon their persons the evidence of the conflict. A leading Whig journal of Illinois (the Quincy *Whig*) says: "As one of the brave defenders of Wisconsin in times that tried the courage of the best men, Dodge stands deservedly among the foremost. His name, his fame, his public acts, are interwoven with the Territory."

The Hon. Wm. Medill, member of Congress from Ohio, and afterwards Governor of that State, referring to those times in a speech in the House of Representatives, April 25th, 1842, said:

When the Western frontiers were invaded by the savage hordes of the wilderness, and the progress of civilization retarded for a time by the tomahawk and scalping-knife, who was it that exposed his life and endured extraordinary hardships in defending the home and the fireside of the emigrant? Who was it that met in mortal combat, and arrested the career of the murderous but brave and intrepid Black Hawk? Who commanded the volunteers at the memorable battle of Wisconsin Heights, where sustained on either side by one of his own youthful but gallant sons he occupied the post of danger, and vanquished a superior force with the loss of a single man? Who led on the charge at Bad Axe, and shed such lustre upon the valor of his countrymen at Pecatonica, where not a single man of the enemy survived to relate the incidents of the conflict? The name of General Dodge is identified with the history and glory of the West, and will ever be held in grateful remembrance by a people whom his chivalry and valor have defended from cruelty and death.

The Hon. John Reynolds, Governor of Illinois in 1832, who was with the troops of that State in the Black Hawk War, and afterwards member of Congress from that State, related in the House of Representatives, on the 9th day of July, 1842, the same incidents mentioned by Senator McRoberts; he says of Henry Dodge:

His character and standing is well-known in the West and throughout the country. I have been intimately acquainted with his career for more than forty years. He was born in the West, and has by the force of native intellect and energy of character sustained himself through various difficulties and trials incident to the settlement of a new country. He has by merit raised himself to a pinnacle of fame, which not frequently falls to the lot of any man to attain. He sustained well in the Black Hawk War the high standing he had previously acquired as a military man.

NOTE.— We are indebted to the Hon. George W. Jones, under date of Nov. 25th, 1889, for the following additional particulars of events referred to in this article:

Mr. St. Vrain was murdered by a war party some thirty miles east of Galena, when on his way, under Gen. Atkinson's orders, to Rock Island from Dixon, via Galena, with six other men, one of whom, my worthy and honored friend, Frederick Stahl, is now living at Galena.

My friend, Hon. Thomas McKnight, then the U. S. Agent of the Lead Mines at Galena, afterwards Receiver of Public Monies at Dubuque, sent a message to me at my then residence and fort at Sinsinawa Mound, that my brother-in-law had either been killed or taken prisoner by the Indians. I immediately mounted my horse, in my buckskin hunting shirt, Kentucky jeans pantaloons, and put out for the rescue of my brother-in-law and his companions, having my double-barrelled gun, well loaded with buck-shot, a holster of pistols, and two in my belt, with a bowie-knife.

I reached Galena several hours after the Cavalry Company of Capt. Stephenson had left for the scene of murder or captivity. Contrary to the entreaty of my friends, Capt. James May, in particular, Mr. McKnight, Major Charles S. Hempstead, and others, I followed on *alone*, and overtook the troop of horse some 25 or 30 miles east of Galena, where I also found Col. Dodge with his mining regiment. In the course of the day the mutilated body of Mr. St. Vrain was found by myself; Col. Dodge and I were the only persons there who had known him. His head, feet, and hands had been cut off, and with his heart and the most of the flesh of his body had been taken off by the Indians as trophies of war, and as food, he being a pretty fat man. We were directed to his corpse by the turkey buzzards which we saw flying and circling around at a considerable distance. I knew him from the color of his black hair, some of which was strewn around as the Indians scalped him, his blue dress coat, swallow-tailed, through the large collar of which, then the style, the bullet which had broken his neck had passed. His pocket-book and papers and the silver and gold money were untouched in his pockets. His head, heart, feet and hands were taken to the headquarters of the Indians, then near Lake Koshkonong, and used in their war dances; one brave having his head swung between his knees, two others a hand each, and two the feet, to brandish. The heart was cut into small pieces, and given to the young boys to swallow, he to be declared the bravest who could gulp down the largest piece.

Mr. St. Vrain rode a splendid horse, and could easily have made a good escape, but he tried hard to hold his horse in and turn him around, but the yelling and warwhoops and screaming of the pursuing Indians on horseback, some forty of them, so frightened his horse and the horses of his companions as to make them unmanageable. The most of these particulars I got from Madame Mayotte,[1] a French interpretess, whom I saw when Col. Dodge rescued the Hall young ladies.

A few days after that meeting with Col. Dodge and his command, he sent his valiant son, Henry L., and his adjutant, W. W. Woodbridge, to my residence and fort at Sinsinawa Mound, to request me to become his aid-de-camp, he having been ordered by the Commander-in-Chief, Gen. Atkinson, to take command of Gen. Posey's brigade of Illinois Volunteers, then encamped near Hamilton's fort. Capt. H. L. Dodge and Adjutant Woodbridge reached my house in the night, after a hard day's ride from Dodgeville. The next morning at daylight I gladly went off with them, accoutred as before, to accept the highest and most responsible office I had ever expected to fill, and under him whom I had loved from my childhood. Col. Dodge was waiting for me to accompany him to take command of some 1,500 volunteers from Southern Illinois. He was in his buckskin, sassafras tanned, hunting shirt, and Kentucky jeans pants, just like my own. As soon as I entered his log cabin residence, having but one window, and no plank but a dirt floor, he welcomed me heartily, and said: "I have sent for you to become my aid-de-camp, because I have unbounded confidence in your friendship, bravery and honor, as I had in your learned and brave father, your brothers, and your brothers-in-law, Hon. John and Judge Andrew Scott, all of whom served under me in the war with Great Britain and their Indian allies, in and on the frontiers of Missouri Territory, in the war of 1812. Your venturing *alone* through the wilderness in search of Mr. St. Vrain and party, was a hazardous undertaking; but it gratified me."

---

1 A half breed, very popular with her tribe, the Winnebagoes. Mrs. Adele P. Gratiot's Narrative, in Wis. Coll., x. 267, 269.

On our arrival at the encampment, Col. Dodge refused to assume command unless the volunteers would elect him as their commander, over their own General; although Col. Davenport, of the U. S. Army, was present, under orders from Gen. Atkinson to make the transfer or substitution in the command. All of the volunteers were entire strangers to Col. Dodge. At his request they were drawn up into a hollow square, when he addressed them, and was followed by Gen. Posey, who appealed to his old neighbors not to desert and disgrace him. His entreaties had the desired effect.

As Col. Dodge and I rode up to Posey's encampment, he pointed out to me the clump of hazle and other bushes in which those thirteen Indians were concealed, waiting for him, as he rode alone on his way to Fort Hamilton, a short time before. That clump was in the angle of a right angle triangle, the hypothenuse of which he took to save time, instead of keeping on the big wagon road.

I attended the treaty made by General Winfield Scott on the Mississippi river directly opposite Rock Island, and procured through my influence with George Davenport, Antoine LeClaire, and the then made chief of the Sac and Fox Nation, Keokuk, two thousand acres of land as an indemnity to the widow and children of Mr. Felix St. Vrain.

III.

MAJOR U. S. MOUNTED RANGERS, 1832-3.

While the Black Hawk war was raging, Congress authorized the creation of a battalion of Mounted Rangers, by Act of June 15th, 1832, for the better protection of the frontiers. In supporting the measure in the House of Representatives, Hon. Joseph Duncan, afterwards Governor of Illinois, said that about the first proposition he ever submitted for the consideration of Congress was one for raising eight companies of mounted gunmen for this service in 1828; he believed that all the distress and bloodshed that had just been heard of in Illinois would have been avoided if Congress had adopted that plan; no number of U. S. soldiers on foot could restore confidence to the citizens residing in that country; families who have witnessed the shocking scenes which had just been acted on the frontier would never return to their homes until an efficient force was raised for their protection; he believed we should hear of no more Indian wars after this force was organized and placed in service. The President appointed Henry Dodge

Major of the battalion. His commission was brought to him by express at the mouth of the Whitewater river, when at the head of his command in line of battle.

As soon as the Black Hawk war was over, a Rangers' camp was established on the Mississippi near the mouth of Rock river. The cholera, which had been brought from the seaboard with the troops under General Scott,[1] broke out in the camp, and raged for three weeks. Thirteen of the Rangers died, and were buried in the woods without coffins. Upon this outbreak of the epidemic General Scott issued the following order:

ASSISTANT ADJUTANT GENERAL'S OFFICE, }
FORT ARMSTRONG, August 28th, 1832. }

Order No. 16.

1. The cholera has made its appearance on Rock Island. The two first cases were brought by mistake from Capt. Ford's company of U. S. Rangers; one of these died yesterday, the other is convalescent. A second death occurred this morning in the hospital in Fort Armstrong. The man was of the 4th Infantry, and had been some time there under treatment for debility. The Ranger now convalescent was in the same hospital with him for sixteen hours before a cholera hospital could be established outside the camp and Fort.

2. It is believed that all these men were of intemperate habits. The Ranger, who is dead, it is known, generated the disease within him by a fit of intoxication.

3. This disease having appeared among the Rangers, and on this Island, all in commission are called upon to exert themselves to the utmost to stop the spread of the calamity.

4. Sobriety, cleanliness of person, cleanliness of camp and quarters, together with care in the preparation of the men's messes, are the grand preventives. No neglect under these important heads will be overlooked or tolerated.

5. In addition to the foregoing, the Senior Surgeon present recommends the use of flannel shirts, flannel drawers and woolen stockings; but the Commanding General, who has seen much of disease, knows that it is *intemperance* which in the present state of the atmosphere generates and spreads the calamity, and that, when once spread, good and temperate men are likely to take the infection.

6. He therefore peremptorily commands that every soldier or Ranger, who shall be found drunk or sensibly intoxicated after the publication of this order, be compelled, as soon as his strength will permit, to dig a grave at a suitable

---

[1] Of about fifteen hundred officers and men of the regular troops ordered to the northwestern frontier, not less than two hundred died by the cholera. Report of the Secretary of War, Nov. 25, 1832.

burying place large enough for his own reception, as such grave cannot fail soon to be wanted for the drunken man himself or some drunken companion.

7. This **Order** is given, as well to serve for the punishment of drunkenness as to spare **good** and temperate men the labor of digging graves for their **worthless** companions.

S. The sanitary regulations now in force respecting communications between the camp near the mouth of Rock river and other camps and posts in the neighborhood are **revoked.** [They had provided for sending all the sick to the hospital on Rock Island]. Col. Eustis, however, whose troops are perfectly free from cholera, will report to the Commanding General whether he believes it for the safety of his command that these regulations should be renewed.   By **order of** MAJOR GENERAL SCOTT,

                                 P. H. GALT, Ass't Adjutant General.

At this time there were three Sacs confined in the military prison at Fort Armstrong on a charge of having been parties to a murderous attack upon a Menominee camp near Prairie du Chien, on the 31st of July, 1831. On account of the cholera Gen. Scott set them at liberty, taking their promise to return upon the exhibition of a certain signal to be hung from the limb of a dead tree at an elevated point of the island when the epidemic should be over. They kept their word, and reported themselves upon the exhibition of the signal. They were again placed on parole, and subsequently released.[1]

ASST. ADJT. GENERAL'S OFFICE, NORTHWESTERN ARMY,
Special Order: ROCK ISLAND, September 6th, 8 2.

The General commanding directs the use of the following paroles and countersigns for the ensuing eight days:

			Parole.	*Countersign.*
1832, Sept.		7.	Cæsar.	Gaul.
		8.	Hannibal.	Capua.
		9.	Napoleon.	Corsica.
		10.	Desaix.	Marengo.
		11.	Saladin.	Palestine.
		12.	Hamlet.	Denmark.
		13.	Atkinson.	Bad Axe.
		14.	Dodge.	Quisconsin.

By order of MAJOR GENERAL SCOTT,

                     R. BACHE,[2] Ass't Adjutant General.

To MAJOR HENRY DODGE,
Commanding Battalion U. S. Rangers,
    Camp on Rock River.

---

1 Autobiography of Lt. General Scott, Chap. xviii.
2 Richard Bache was a descendant of Benjamin Franklin.

Major Dodge was present at the treaty made by General Scott and Governor Reynolds with the Winnebagoes, on Rock Island, on the 15th of September and at the request of those Indians acted as their friend and adviser in the Council. Writing a number of years afterward, Gen. Scott spoke of that occasion and of the course of Henry Dodge in the Black Hawk war, in the following manner:

In the Black Hawk war Gen. Dodge displayed, as was generally acknowledged, the greatest vigor in pursuit, and prowess in conflict with the Indians. After Gen. Atkinson's battle of the Bad Axe, the Western Army came under my immediate command, and I know that Gen. Dodge was held in the highest dread by both the enemy and their secret abettors, the Winnebagoes. Yet, at the treaty held with the latter, Gen. Dodge was chosen as their councillor, and it gave me great delight to witness the zeal and humanity he displayed in protecting their interests, a trait, in my humble judgment, as honorable to him as his victorious blade. I was upon the whole deeply impressed with his merits and have not since doubted that according to their merits, or demerits, he will ever be found the protector or punisher of the Indians about him.[1]

He was also present at the "treaty of peace, friendship, and cession," made on the 21st of September with the Sacs and Foxes, upon the site of the present city of Davenport. His signature was appended as a witness to both treaties. These treaties were of great historical significance to the future State of Iowa. That with the Winnebagoes granted to them what was then known as the "Neutral Ground," in what is now Northern Iowa, in lieu of lands they had long occupied on the east side of the Mississippi, south and east of the Wisconsin river and of Fox river of Green Bay. By the treaty with the Sacs and Foxes, those confederated tribes ceded to the U. S. "a tract of the Sac and Fox country bordering on the invaded frontier, more than proportional to the numbers of the hostile band that had been conquered and subdued," viz., a strip of land on the east side of the Mississippi, about two hundred miles in length, extending from the boundary line of the State of Missouri on the south to the "Neutral Ground" on the north, and ranging from fifty to seventy-five miles in breadth, containing about six million acres of land; and they agreed to

---

1 Letter of Winfield Scott to A. C. Dodge, Feb. 9th, 1841.

remove from the ceded country on or before the first day of
June, 1833, with the express understanding that they were
not to reside, plant, fish, or hunt on any portion of it after that
date. Thus that date became memorable in Iowa history
as the day in which a portion of her territory first became
open to occupation and settlement by the American people.

The battalion of mounted Rangers consisted of six companies, three of which (Captains James D. Henry, Benjamin
V. Beekes, and Jesse B. Browne[1]) were assigned by Major
General Scott to the Northwestern frontier, to range between
the Wabash river, Chicago, Ft. Winnebago, and the mouth of
the Wisconsin river, under the immediate instructions of Major
Dodge. The other companies (Captains Lemuel Ford, Jesse
Bean, and Nathan Boone[1]) were ordered to Fort Gibson, on
the Arkansas river, for the protection of the Southwestern
frontier. The circumstances and discipline of the service are
explained in the following orders of Major Dodge:

RANGERS CAMP NEAR ROCK ISLAND, }
September 23d, 1832. }

Order No. 9.

Capt. Browne will march his company from his present encampment to the
vicinity of Danville, Illinois. He is permitted to make a proper selection of a
position for erecting suitable buildings for the use of his officers and men for
the next winter. In the choice of this position he will select the most suitable
place for fuel, as well as forage for the horses; it being an object of the first
importance that the corn and forage should be as cheap as possible.

The greatest respect is to be paid to the private rights of citizens. The
Rangers were intended for the defence and protection of the inhabitants of the
frontiers, and it is strictly enjoined on each officer and Ranger not to trespass
on the private rights of any citizen without paying a just equivalent for what
may be received.

Gambling and drinking to intoxication is prohibited. The Captain commanding will order court martials for the trial of those found intoxicated, and
punish them without delay; as well as prevent gambling in his camp.

Capt. Browne will report to me monthly, to be directed to Mineral Point,

---

1 Capt. Browne was a member from Lee County of the Council of the first
four Legislative Assemblies of Iowa Territory, of the H. of R. of the 8th
Legislative Assembly, and of the H. of R. and Speaker of the House, of the
First General Assembly of the State. Capt. Boone was a son of Daniel
Boone, the Kentucky pioneer. A sketch of their lives is in the Annals of
Iowa, July, 1872, pp 196, 226.

Michigan Territory, the strength and condition of his company, as to arms, ammunition, provisions, as well as the state and condition of his horses.

The Commanding Officer of the Rangers expects that each officer and Ranger will be prompt and diligent in the discharge of his duty. The government intends this corps as the **vanguard** for the frontier This high expectation must not be disappointed.

VANDALIA, ILL., October 13th, 1832.

Capt. Jesse Browne,
Commanding a Company of U. S. Rangers:

I have this day received a letter from His Excellency, Governor Reynolds, stating that the Pottawattamie Indians had assumed an imposing and threatening attitude on the northern frontier of Illinois. From the pressing manner the Governor writes me on this subject, you will without delay march your company from the vicinity of Danville to the northern frontier of this State. You will range the country from Ottawa at the mouth of Fox river on the Illinois river, so as to completely cover the settlements on Beaver creek in the counties of Putnam and La Salle. You will order the Pottawattamies out of the settlements, and drive them out of the range of the settlements, if they refuse to go. You will select such a position on Bureau as will enable you to procure corn and forage for your horses. Your assistant commissary will make the necessary purchases for the supply of the company, unless the company should find it more convenient to furnish themselves. You are not to make an attack on the Pottawattamies unless they should make an attack on the frontiers. Should they, however, shed a drop of white blood, you will not hesitate to kill the offenders, their aiders and abettors. Should the Indians leave that frontier, and the minds of the inhabitants be quieted, you will return to your winter quarters near Danville. You will exercise your own judgment as to the proper time to leave the frontier, which will be governed wholly by the attitude assumed by the Indians.

Early in 1833 Henry Dodge visited Washington. Regarded as the hero of the Black Hawk war, he was received with marked attention and honor. President Andrew Jackson greeted him with assurances of high appreciation and esteem. Senator Buckner, of Missouri, complimented him in the Senate chamber, as already quoted. Those were the squally days of nullification in South Carolina. Gen. Scott had been ordered to Charleston, also ships of war, and the President had signified his determination, if matters grew worse, to appoint Henry Dodge Marshal of South Carolina, to insure the execution of the laws of the United States in that State. The following letter to Henry Dodge, from his half-brother, Lewis F. Linn, M. D., who, upon the death of Mr. Buckner by cholera the next summer, succeeded him as Senator from Missouri, relates to this period:

SAINTE GENEVIEVE, February 15th, 1833.

DEAR BROTHER:—I had written you a few days before the reception of your letter announcing your arrival at Washington. It is needless for me to say how much I was gratified at the friendly and distinguished manner of your reception by our venerable and truly great President, so every way qualified to judge of the relative merit of men. How contemptible his revilers must feel on seeing him every moment growing in greatness and increasing in the confidence and affection of the American people! Time, you know, is an indolent old fellow not fond of burthens, and, as he drives along the stream into the ocean of eternity, freighted with the reputation of men, is ever and anon engaged in selecting from his overloaded bark such as do not deserve immortality, and casting them into oblivion. Among the retained will ever be found the name of Andrew Jackson.

Your chivalrous conduct during the late Indian war has truly placed you on elevated ground, from whence you will be enabled to catch a glimpse of coming events, and turn them to your advantage and to that of our common country. It would be a sincere source of regret to find in our domestic troubles you might be compelled to shed American blood, but if stern necessity requires it I know your valor will be tempered with humanity. In a government like ours, made by the people and for the people, where the public will is the supreme arbiter, where the great mass of the people seldom err in judgment, every friend to his country, nay, every friend to liberty throughout the world, may still entertain a reasonable hope that the difficulty with South Carolina will yet be arranged without a resort to force; but should it be otherwise I entertain no fear for the result, and none that you will conduct yourself, if engaged, in such a way as to benefit your country, and add to your well-earned reputation.

In accordance with your wish I will write Col. Buckner, happy if any little influence I may possess could be of service to you; but I doubt much if he has weight at Washington. You know the President, and, knowing him, you can judge whether his wavering course heretofore is likely to gain him the esteem of General Jackson, whose judgment is so unerring as regards men; in fact his election was the result of a singular combination of circumstances, most of which Col. Benton is acquainted with. I might have been in his place, if I had not disdained to be elected by my political opponents; even if I was considered of sufficient importance to be bid for. I had to choose between him and Wells, and I preferred Buckner, knowing that the southern part of the State had in some measure been overlooked heretofore. I must say he has shown every disposition to befriend me since. His subsequent opposition to Col. Benton is, I presume, part of the price he had to pay the Clay men for their support. In this I was completely deceived, or he would not have received my vote.

I am aware of the many virtues of Gen. Ashley, of his sterling good sense, and of his sincere unfeigned friendship for you; but, my dear brother, Col.

Benton is the only man Missouri ever had in Congress whose splendid talents, unwavering purpose of soul, and expanded views entitled him to the character of a great man. It would not surprise me to see him President. At present I view Richard M. Johnson as the only man that stands between him and Vice-President. In support of him last summer, patriotism and personal regard were combined to induce me to contribute my mite toward his success. He ever to me manifested a sincere friendship for you, and for myself I owe him many acts of kindness.

My constitution is much worn out by sickness and a harrassing profession; my head is tolerably well sprinkled with gray hairs, great muscular debility from palpitation of the heart, though I weigh what my father did when he died, 180 pounds. I endeavor to fulfil my duty to my profession, country, friends, and family, and will try to live without fear and die without reproach. After my time as Commissioner expires, I would be pleased to get some appointment for which I might be qualified, that would relieve me from this unfortunate profession of mine to be looking always on man as an object of affliction and sorrow, to be compelled to examine him by piecemeal, every tendon, muscle, bone, nerve, and organ, but worst of all to be compelled to analyze his passions, trace them to their source, and view them in their naked deformity; my soul yearns after getting rid of this.

I have at present three fine children; my wife's health very bad; our old friend Scott is much under the weather; he appears to delight in your brightening prospects; sister is as usual, happy and cheerful; nothing can crush her fortitude; our town and section of country looking up. That your visit to Washington may be one of pleasure and profit is the sincere wish of your brother. L. F. LINN.[1]

GEN. H. DODGE.

In his annual report, November 25th, 1832, the Secretary of War, Mr. Cass, recommended the conversion of the corps of rangers into a regiment of dragoons. Consequent upon this recommendation, an act for the more perfect defence of the frontiers was passed by Congress, approved March 2d, 1833. It provided for a regiment of ten companies, of one hundred men each. The President appointed Henry Dodge Colonel of the regiment. Thus honored with the confidence of the Government, Col. Dodge returned to his command. He

---

1 Dr. Linn was at this time one of three Commissioners to settle Spanish land claims in Missouri. His sister, Mrs. Mary Ann McArthur, removed to Michigan Territory in 1835, and kept hotel at Belmont during the first session of the First Legislative Assembly of Wisconsin Territory, 1836. Gen. Ashley was member of House of Representatives from Missouri. John Scott was delegate to Congress from Missouri Territory, 1817-1821

issued the following order to one of his Captains, who had been appointed in the place of Capt. Henry.

ST. LOUIS, March 31st, 1833.

Capt. Matthew Duncan,[1]
   Commanding Company of U. S. Rangers:

You will on hearing of the departure of the caravans for Santa Fe hold your company in readiness, and march them to join the caravans at the nearest point from your present encampment. Your command will act as an escort until you arrive at the Arkansas river, or the boundary line between the United States and Mexico. You will afford the caravans on their march all the aid and assistance in your power, and defend them against the attack of the hostile Indians. You will preserve the utmost harmony between the Rangers and the Santa Fe traders. On your march you will guard against the possibility of surprise. On your arrival at the southwestern boundary line of the United States, you will have an express understanding with the traders as to the time they will return, and you will meet them with your company on their return at the boundary line, and act as an escort until they pass the line of the State of Missouri.   H. DODGE,

Col. U. S. Dragoons, Commanding U. S. Rangers.

Upon the Illinois frontier he found the people in a state of alarm from a wide-spread apprehension that the Winnebagoes and Pottawattamies were forming a combination to attack the settlements. He at once made a disposition of troops to quiet the public mind and protect the frontier. A low stage of water in the river preventing steamboats from passing the rapids of the Upper Mississippi, he travelled on horseback from St. Louis by way of Vandalia, Fort Clark and Dixon's Ferry to Dodgeville, a distance of 400 miles. The following letters explain the condition of the frontier at this period:

VANDALIA, April 3d, 1833.

To Captains Beekes and Browne.

The threatening attitude of the Winnebagoes and the exposed situation of our Northwestern frontier makes it important for the safety of the citizens of that frontier, as well as to enforce a strict observance of the treaty made with the Winnebagoes, that you should march from your present position to Hennepin on the Illinois river, to arrive at that place by the 20th of April, if possible. Supplies for the Rangers will be sent up the Illinois river to that place by Gen. Atkinson. On your arrival at Hennepin, you will immediately report to me near Dodgeville, Michigan Territory. It is important that your move-

---

1   M. Duncan was publisher of the first newspaper in Illinois, the Illinois *Herald*, at Kaskaskia. He was a brother of Joseph Duncan, Governor of Illinois, 1834-S.

ment should be made promptly. At Hennepin you will be about sixty miles from Rock river, where you can march immediately to Rock river, or any other part of the country where it may be necessary to concentrate the Rangers.

DIXON'S FERRY, April 9th, 1833.

To Gen. Atkinson, St. Louis:

I arrived at this place at 10 o'clock last night, accompanied by Mr. Wood-bridge, after a ride of seventy miles. I found the people moving in every direction, much excited. There are no **families** on the road from Meredith, twenty miles this side of **Fort Clark, except Thomas, and none between this** place and Apple **river.** The information received through **Dixon has directly operated** on the great mass of the community living **on this frontier. From his statements** the conduct of the Winnebagoes is mysterious and doubtful. A short time will determine the course they will take. Lieutenant Wilson, of the U. S. Army, is going directly to Jefferson Barracks; he is from the mines, and can inform you as to the state of public feeling. It is **certainly** desirable that the Government should purchase as early as possible the Pottawattamie coun-try,[1] and enforce the treaty made with the **Winnebagoes. Such is the state of feeling of the people, that the Indians** must be removed to prevent war, the sooner the better.

Should the Indians make any hostile movements, I will endeavor to be pre-pared for them. Their inquiries have been very particular where I was, and where my family were. I will advise the people of the mining country to form themselves into mounted companies, as many as can procure horses, and will post myself with them in advance of the settlements, if there is an appear-ance of danger. I will see Gratiot on my way home, and will send for the principal chiefs of the Winnebagoes, and have a talk with them, which I will communicate to you.

NEAR DODGEVILLE, MICH. TY., April 13th, 1833.

To Major General Macomb,
Commanding U. S. Army at Washington City:

The inhabitants of the **Illinois** frontier appear in much dread from an attack of the **Pottawattamies, and** are leaving the settlements; many of them I met in wagons. They appear in great dread of a premeditated attack from both Pottawattamies and Winnebagoes. I am convinced **that** nothing short of an extinguishment of the title of the Pottawattamies **to the country** bordering on the State of Illinois, and their removal from that frontier, will quiet the minds of the inhabitants. I consider it important to the future growth of this

---

1 The Pottawattamie country contained about **five** millions of acres lying along the **western** shore of Lake Michigan, **and** between that lake and the land lately ceded **to** the U. S. by the Winnebagoes. **By** a treaty made a few months afterward at Chicago it was ceded to the U. S. September 26th, 1833, and the Pottawattamies agreed to remove to the country now constituting a part of Southwestern Iowa and of Northwestern Missouri, lying between the Boyer and Nodaway rivers, and embracing five millions of acres. *U. S. Statutes at Large, vii, 431.*

country that the Winnebagoes should be forced to leave the country they have ceded to the U. S., and that there should be a separation of the Winnebagoes and Pottawattamies. Such is the dislike of the people of the frontier generally of these two nations, impressed as they are with the belief that they participated in the late war with the Sacs and Foxes, that war must be the inevitable result unless they are all removed. Whether the inhabitants are in danger or not, they appear confident of the hostile disposition of these Indians. I have seen Mr. Gratiot, sub agent, since my arrival. He says no danger is to be apprehended from the Winnebagoes, that they say they will not go to war with the whites, but that they wish to remain on the lands they have ceded to the U. S., and raise corn, and that when they receive their annuity money in the fall they will cross the Wisconsin river to their country. This arrangement will not suit the people of this frontier. Nothing but the removal of the Rock River Indians will satisfy the people; and from the advantages the Indians have, their knowledge of the country, the extent of the swamps, as well as the thickets and fallen timber where they could secrete themselves and be free from an attack of a body of horses, unless the Winnebagoes go peaceably it will take at least 700 mounted men to remove them to act on foot or mounted, as this particular service may require.

Gratiot states to me he saw among the Winnebagoes four of the murderers that made their escape from Fort Winnebago last fall.[1] If they are as friendly as they profess to be, why not give up the murderers? It would certainly be the best evidence of their disposition to act correctly. The people of the mining country are satisfied of the guilt of the Winnebagoes in having aided the Sacs in the war against us and the escape of the Winnebago murderers. It being known to all that the murderers of our people are protected by the great body of the Winnebagoes on Rock river will make it difficult to keep peace unless these murderers are given up.

DODGEVILLE, April 22d, 1833.

To Brigadier General H. Atkinson,
Commanding the Right Wing of the Western Dept., U. S. Army:

On my arrival at Gratiot's Grove on the 10th inst., I proposed to Mr. Gratiot, who had returned from the Turtle village the evening before, to send immediately for the chiefs of the Winnebagoes on Rock river. My object was to ascertain the state of feeling among them. Mr. Gratiot states that they deny any hostile feelings towards the whites, and that they have no ammunition, and are almost in a state of starvation.

Mr. John Kinzie, sub-agent at Fort Winnebago, was with me last night; he is directly from that place by the way of Daugherty's, an Indian trader, who

---

1 These murderers were charged, some of them, with the murder of St. Vrain, in Illinois, others with the murder of Aubrey, Green, and Force, near the Blue Mounds. They made their escape from the black hole at the fort, by digging under the stone foundation with their knives through the earth, a distance of seven or eight feet outside the fort. *Niles' Register, January 19th, 1833.*

is settled near the Four Lakes. He says the Winnebagoes are in great dread of the whites, and wish much to see me. I have agreed to meet Kinzie at the Four Lakes on this day week. He will notify the Indians, and will attend. I will endeavor to have Gratiot present, and Pauquette as interpreter. I will let the Indians know the necessity of their removal.

Mr. Kinzie states, on his return from Chicago recently, that he had seen and talked with Caldwell, the chief of the Pottawattamies, who says they are anxious to sell their country to the United States and move west of the Mississippi; and that they are anxious to explore the country west of the Mississippi, and want an escort of Rangers to accompany them, as the country west of the Mississippi is owned by different nations of Indians, with the exception of that portion recently purchased by the United States from the Sacs and Foxes. A treaty would have to be made with the Indians owning the country they might select, before their removal could be effected.

I received a letter from Capt. Beekes, dated from his camp near Vincennes on the 9th inst. He acknowledges the receipt of my order. He appears to think it will be impossible for him to reach Hennepin by the 20th inst. He states that Paymaster Philips had not arrived, that the Rangers were without money to buy forage for their horses, that he had selected Mr. Samuel Smith to purchase rations for the Rangers as well as forage for their horses, and was busily engaged in making the necessary preparations for their march, that he would reach Hennepin as early as possible, that the health of the men was good, their horses in excellent order, and that they were well armed and equipped for service.

Capt. Browne will, I presume, be at Hennepin with his company by the time specified. I have no doubt the Rangers of these companies will be employed on this frontier during their term of enlistment. Supplies of provisions will be wanting for them at some convenient points, say Fort Winnebago, Fort Crawford, and at Helena, on the Wisconsin river. It is believed that the Winnebagoes will locate themselves at or near the old Sac village. Helena would be a central point between the Portage and the mouth of the Wisconsin river, and, as the Winnebagoes will be all removed north of the river, there will be no necessity for ranging the country on the Rock river, unless it should be necessary to watch the movements of the Pottawattamies on the Illinois frontier.

I will immediately, after a meeting with the Winnebagoes, forward you copies of our talk with them. The large amount now to be paid the Winnebagoes annually, and the conflicting interests of agents as well as Indian traders, make it difficult to come at the truth.

NEAR DODGEVILLE, April 25th, 1833.

Capt. Jesse Browne,

Commanding a Company of U. S. Rangers:

I received your favor of the 20th inst. from Hennepin by express. Your arrival at that place was calculated to quiet the minds of the inhabitants on the Illinois frontier; the people have been kept in a state of agitation from conflicting reports.

With a view to ensuring the complete execution of the treaty with the Winnebagoes, I am directed to order your company to advance as early as the season will permit, to take such a position as will enable your command to be effective in reference to the removal of the Winnebagoes, should they hesitate to comply with the treaty.

To facilitate the views of the Government, you will march your company to this frontier as early as possible, and as the supplies of provisions, arms and ammunition for the use of your company must be drawn at Fort Crawford, you will have to draw at least ten days rations at Hennepin; the distance from that place to Fort Crawford is 200 miles. As it will be necessary for me to communicate with Col. Taylor, the commanding officer at Fort Crawford, you will pass near my residence in the mining country, which is the direct route from Rock river to Fort Crawford, and report to me for further orders.

I am to hold a talk with the chiefs of the Rock River Band of Winnebagoes at the Four Lakes on the 29th. inst., and will possibly get some information that may be depended on. From the statements of the Indian Agents it would seem the Winnebagoes are in great dread of an attack from the Rangers this spring. I will communicate to them what the views of the Government are as respects their removal from the lands they have ceded to the United States. I have no doubt it is absolutely necessary for the security of the frontier inhabitants both of Illinois and Michigan that the Pottawattamies and Winnebagoes should be separated, and that they should be obliged to leave their present residence.

Similar orders to those sent to Capt. Browne were sent to Capt. Beekes. Col. Dodge met the Winnebago chiefs at the Four Lakes on the 29th of April, as is described in the following letters:

May 2d, 1833.

Brigadier General Atkinson:

I forward you a copy of the talk held with the Winnebagoes at the head of the Four Lakes on the 29th ult. Mr. Kinzie attended the council as well as Mr. Gratiot; Pauquette acted as interpreter. The White Crow and Whirling Thunder were anxious that I should speak first, no doubt with a view of ascertaining if any advantage could be taken on their part. I told the chiefs I wished to know what their feelings and wishes were in relation to removal from the country they had ceded the United States last year. I replied to the talk of the chiefs, and then told them I would be glad to hear from them again. They made no reply to that part of my talk in relation to the murderers.

From all the information I can procure, the traders and some others have told the Indians that as they delivered the murderers once, and the whites permitted them to escape, by the laws of nations the whites would have to retake them.

I was informed about four days before I met the Indians in council, that one hundred and fifty of the Winnebagoes had been at Daugherty's trading house, which is about fifteen miles from the Four Lakes, to see me, understanding I was to be there at that time. The Indian who killed St. Vrain, the Indian agent, was among the number, dressed very fine, and said he wanted to see me. Some steps should be taken to oblige the chiefs to deliver these murderers. I have received no instructions on that subject. I discovered a great unwillingness on the part of the Indians to leave the country they have sold the United States. Nothing but a strong mounted force will drive them off. My opinion is, a few of the leading men will go to save appearances, and many will remain on the Upper Rock river, which is so well calculated to afford them shelter and protection.

I had the honor of receiving your favor of the 15th ult. I had not intended organizing the militia of the mining country unless the hostile disposition of the Indians was apparent. I am much gratified that the steps I have taken in calling the Indians into council has met your approbation. I could devise no plan that appeared to me more advisable than to call them together, and have their agents present at a conference with them.

I am exceedingly unwilling to assume responsibilities not warranted by the express letter of my orders. I have, however, frequently from necessity and not choice been obliged to act from circumstances. As this frontier is under your immediate direction I should not act without your orders as the commanding general, except in cases of great apparent danger:

NEAR DODGEVILLE, M. T., May 3d, 1833.

Hon. Lewis Cass, Secretary of War:

[After communicating the same information as is contained in the above letter to Gen. Atkinson] . . . . . You are much better acquainted with the Indian character than I can pretend to be, and can form more correct conclusions than I can. The Winnebagoes are the most difficult Indians to understand I have ever been acquainted with. If they could avoid a compliance with their engagements to leave the country they have ceded to the United States, they would do so. The Rangers will be here in a few days. Whether the two companies will be a force sufficiently imposing to oblige the Upper Rock River Winnebagoes to remove, I am unable to say. A few of the leading men I think will remove; but it is doubtful whether the major part of them will cross the Wisconsin river. Their chiefs appear to have less influence over them than any Indians I have known.

Upon the arrival of the two companies of Rangers at Col. Dodge's headquarters the latter part of May, they were ordered, after halting a week, to take a position suitable for camping in the neighbohood of the Four Lakes, in order to watch the Winnebagoes, and to insure their strict observance of the treaty made with them at Rock Island. They established a camp near the northwest side of Fourth Lake, and named it Belle Fountain; and subsequently a camp on the

Wisconsin river, and named it camp Knox. Supplies of ammunition and subsistence were drawn from Fort Winnebago, and from Helena, on the Wisconsin river. The two companies were under the command of Capt. Beekes, to whom Col. Dodge gave the following orders, June 4th:

Captain Beekes will observe a mild but decided course towards the Winnebagoes. He will order a detachment of twenty men under the command of an officer, who will take the main trail of the Sacs to where they crossed the muddy fork of Rock river; after crossing that branch of Rock river they will take the main trail made by the whites to where the volunteers under my command reached Rock river from Fort Winnebago. By this movement you will ascertain if a part of the Winnebagoes are yet remaining on Rock river. You will keep detachments ranging the country to Whitewater on the Rock river, as well as to the Turtle village formerly occupied by the Winnebagoes, and ascertain, if possible, if any part of the Winnebagoes have removed to the lands of the Pottawattamies. Should you find a considerable number of the Winnebagoes yet remaining on the lands they have ceded the United States, you will immediately send an express to Col. Taylor, commanding at Fort Crawford, under whose orders you are placed during my absence to the southern frontier, and no steps are to be taken until his arrival, as the removal of the Winnebagoes devolves exclusively on Col. Taylor, should they refuse to leave the country agreeably to the stipulations of the treaty made at Rock Island.

Should the U. S. Rangers meet the Winnebagoes, or find them located on the ceded lands, they are to take no steps, but report the facts to the commanding officer of the detachment, unless they should be attacked by the Winnebagoes. In that event they are to kill the offenders, their aiders and abetters, if possible. The parties sent on this service should be directed to be strictly on their guard against the possibility of surprise, by keeping their spies always in the advance and on their flanks and rear such a distance as to give the main party time to be prepared for action, should it become necessary. Silence is of the first importance where there is the possibility of danger; loud talking and laughing should be prohibited on a march; caution is the first duty of a soldier; the utmost vigilance will be necessary in preventing horses from being stolen by the Indians, or straying away; they must be well secured at all times.

Discipline and subordination is of vital importance to all bodies of armed men. The drill for the Rangers as prescribed by the War Department must be practiced each day when the weather will permit; the dismounting motion, linking horses, advancing the Rangers in line, in open order, and at trail arms, is an important movement that should be well understood by the Rangers.

The commanding officer of the Rangers directs that the rules and articles of war shall be observed and obeyed, and that the general regulations of the army be observed in all cases. A proper deference and respect from the officers to each other, it is expected, will be strictly observed in their respective relations. Combining as the officers of this detachment do a knowledge of the leading principles of their profession, as well as a practical knowledge of Indian warfare, the most happy results may be expected in affording protection to the settlers on the frontiers.

Ordered by Gen. Atkinson to make a demand upon the Winnebago chiefs for the murderers who had escaped the previous fall, Col. Dodge made arrangements to meet the chiefs at the Portage for that purpose.

June 4th, 1833.

To Gen. Henry Atkinson:

Yours of the 24th ult. I received this morning. I am much gratified that my course in relation to the Winnebagoes has met your approbation. Every facility has been afforded the Winnebagoes of Rock river to enable them peaceably to leave the country they have ceded to the United States; the corn promised them they have received, and Capt. Gentry hauled their canoes from the Four Lakes to the Wisconsin river. The Whirling Thunder, the Blind or White Crow, Little Priest, Little Black, and White Breast had crossed over to the Wisconsin with their canoes. The Man Eater, who is the principal chief on the Upper Rock river, and the Spotted Arm, it was understood, had not crossed the Wisconsin. Capt. Gentry saw about one hundred men, warriors. From all the information I have been able to procure, not one half of the Rock River Indians have crossed the Wisconsin; and the Indians that have crossed are no doubt waiting to see what steps will be taken as to the removal of those remaining on the lands they have ceded the United States.

I will take a position near the Four Lakes, where I can march to any part of the Rock River country in two days. The large trails made last season will be easily followed by light parties that may be sent out to make discoveries. I have always been of opinion it would require an armed force to drive the Winnebagoes from Rock River. Should a spirit of resistance be shown on the part of the Indians, when I ascertain the probable number I can better determine what number of troops will be necessary to drive them, and will advise you immediately. I will get Pauquette, if possible, to accompany me as interpreter. It will be difficult at present to get the murderers. The course you have advised will be pursued. I have no doubt it will require the action of the chiefs to effect a delivery of them. I will immediately call the attention of the Indian agents to the subject, and meet the chiefs as early as possible. The Portage will be, I think, the better place to convene them.

NEAR DODGEVILLE, June 8th, 1832.

To Brigadier General Atkinson:

I leave this place early to-morrow morning for the Four Lakes. I will ascertain as early as possible the movements of the Winnebagoes, and advise the Indian agents of the time and place I will meet the chiefs to make a demand of the murderers. I learned from Mr. Goodale, sutler at Fort Winnebago, that Mr. Kinzie, the Indian agent at the Portage, had gone to Green Bay, to meet Governor Porter, and that he would not return to the Portage before the 15th inst.

The Four Lakes, I think, will be a proper point to post the Rangers; the
distance from Helena will be about thirty-seven miles. The Rangers have six
wagons, and will be able with convenience to transport the necessary supplies
for their use while at that place, and it will be within fifteen miles of the Wisconsin river, and where I can ascertain better the movements of the Indians,
and range the country from the Blue Mounds to Fort Winnebago.

In addition to his duties with the Rangers in connection
with the removal of the Winnebagoes, Col. Dodge was also
occupied with arrangements for the organization of the Regiment of U. S. Dragoons. The following extracts relate in
part to those arrangements:

DODGEVILLE, June 8th, 1833.

To Major J. B. Brant,
    Quartermaster, **St. Louis, Missouri:**

Every attention shall be paid for the safe keeping of the public horses. It is
desirable. however, they should be removed as early as possible to where they
might be wanting for the use of the Dragoons, as they are in fine order.
Should any of the public horses stray off, or be stolen, I certainly ought not to
be responsible for them.

I am much gratified to hear the public horses purchased by me will be paid
for, and that a settlement will take place for the mounting and equipping the
Iowa County Militia. The responsibility I was obliged to take for the defence
and protection of our frontier has been a source of great uneasiness to me. I
have given to Major Kirby, the paymaster, all the information in my power,
and, if my duties on the frontier will permit me, will do everything I can to
assist Capt. Palmer, Special Agent for the Quartermaster's Department, in his
settlement of the public accounts.

In your letter of the 30th ult., you stated you had received instructions for
the erection of stables, store-houses, and for equipments, etc., for the Regiment
of Dragoons. I fully agree with you in your views as to the propriety of
regarding efficiency and durability in the outfit as essential to the future use-
fulness of the corps, and that economy should be observed in the expenditure
of the public money in the erection of stables.

The Regiment of Dragoons was intended for the more perfect defence of
this frontier. I do not know what the views of the Government may be as to
the future disposition of the Regiment I presume, however, they will be stationed after their organization on the frontier. It is not to be expected that
Jefferson Barracks will be the permanent headquarters of the Regiment longer
than may be necessary to complete its organization.

On his return from Fort Winnebago he forwarded the following report to Gen. Atkinson:

DODGEVILLE, MICHIGAN TY., June 29th, 1833.

GENERAL:—I received your letter of 13th inst. yesterday evening on my
return from Fort Winnebago. On the 9th inst. I started from this place for

.

Fort Winnebago, reached the Rangers' camp near the Four Lakes on the 10th inst., and arrived at Fort Winnebago on the 14th. Mr. Kinzie, sub-agent for the Winnebagoes, arrived on the 15th with twenty thousand dollars, the annuity money for the Winnebagoes. I waited on Mr. Kinzie, and sent for Mr. Pauquette, the interpreter, and had a confidential conference with them on the subject of the removal of the Winnebagoes, as well as the necessity of a prompt delivery of the eight murderers who made their escape from Fort Winnebago last fall; and that a refusal on the part of the Indians to remove from the ceded lands would oblige me to march with the mounted Rangers to drive them across the Wisconsin river, and that it might be necessary for me to call on the Government for aid, and, should it become necessary to do so, that the chiefs would be in danger of being taken and held as hostages until the murderers were delivered up, to be dealt with according to law. I was well apprised that Man Eater, the chief on the Upper Rock river, had not left his village, and that at least sixty lodges were yet remaining on the Upper Rock river. Mr. Kinzie having the annuity money in his possession, I thought it would be a favorable moment to call the attention of the chiefs to this subject, that the annuity money would not be paid them, until they complied with the demands of the Government. I desired Mr. Kinzie to notify the chiefs I would meet them on the 22d inst., at the Portage; in the meantime, the Indians on the Rock river should be all notified, both as to their removal, as well as my course in relation to the murderers.

I left the Rangers on the morning of the 22d inst., and arrived at Fort Winnebago at about 10 o'clock. The Rangers arrived at the fort at about 12 o'clock. I enclose you a talk held with the chiefs:

To the Chiefs of the Winnebago Nation:

When at the Four Lakes, on the 29th of April, in my talk with you I told you that a cloud of darkness would rest on your Nation until you delivered up to justice the eight murderers taken by you last fall under a stipulation of the treaty made with the U. S. Commissioners at Rock Island. You acted in that respect with good faith. The murderers have made their escape; they have received your aid and protection. During the winter on Rock river, your agent, Mr. Gratiot, stated to me he had seen four of them; he identified the Indian who killed the U. S. agent of the Sacs and Foxes, Mr. St. Vrain.

It becomes my duty to demand of you, the chiefs, that these men be delivered to me; their escape from justice is no acquittal of them. Is it right, is it just, that men who professed to be our friends, and when the Government of the U. S. was in a state of peace with their nation, that a part of them should unite with the Sac and Fox Indians, to kill our weak and defenceless citizens on this frontier and charge the crimes on the Sacs? The men who participated in killing the U. S. Indian agent, and his murderer, whom, as Mr. Gratiot, your agent, states, Mr. St. Vrain had fed and extended to him all the rights of hospitality and friendship at his house at Rock Island but two weeks before he was killed!—the Indian who barbarously cut off his hands and feet before his death!—have been permitted by you to go at large, covered with the blood of an innocent man, without any attempt since the escape of these murderers on your part to bring him and the rest of the murderers to that justice their crimes merit. This state of things is in direct violation of every principle of justice; and contrary to all usage among friendly nations, for one party to harbor and conceal murderers and culprits claimed by the other party.

I now distinctly give you to understand that if you fail to adopt measures for the apprehension of the fugitives from justice, it will lead to a stoppage of your annuities by the Government and that your chiefs are liable to be arrested and detained until the delivery of the murderers.

Your great father, the President of the United States, deals justly with all nations, whether a strong or a weak people; he asks nothing of them that is not right; and he will submit to nothing that is wrong. He will do justice to all the Red Skins. Had our frontier people killed any of the

Winnebagoes in a time of peace, they would have been punished according to the laws of the country where the crime was committed. If your people kill ours, they must be punished in the same manner that our citizens are punished. The laws are made for the protection of all, as well as for the punishment of all who violate them.

If you deliver the murderers to us, to be dealt with according to law, you will give us a proof of your friendly disposition, and that you are disposed to observe and conform to those friendly relations that should exist among different nations of people; then the bright chain of friendship will remain entire and unbroken between us.

Should you fail to deliver these murderers, your road will be filled with thorns, and the sun will be covered with a dark cloud, which will rest over your nation until the blood of the innocent is avenged.

Judge Doty, the former U. S. District Judge, now practicing as an attorney, had been at the Portage after my conference with Mr. Kinzie. He had been employed last fall by the murderers to defend them. He advised the friends of the culprits to deliver themselves up to Mr. Kinzie, who was the only acting magistrate at the Portage, before my arrival. As Mr. Kinzie lived in Brown county, the murderers would be committed to the gaol of that county, and they would not be taken to Prairie du Chien and confined, and would not have to be tried in Iowa county, where the alleged murders were committed, and where public opinion was decidedly against them. Mr. Kinzie directed the accused murderers to be placed in the guard house in the fort, under the ninth article of the treaty made at Rock Island. The names of the murderers were given, and three of them were given up as the murderers of Mr. St. Vrain, killed near Kellogg's Grove, in the State of Illinois, who must be tried in that State; and consequently a demand must be made by the Governor of the State of Illinois on the Governor of this Territory for the delivery of the murderers of St. Vrain I mention this subject in order that the proper steps may be taken in relation to the trial of these murderers.

The Indians charged with killing Aubrey, Green, and Force, near the Blue Mounds, must be tried in the county where the murder was committed, unless the Judge orders the change of the venue. The Indians were marching to the fort on my arrival; seven of them have been committed; there is a hostage for the eighth, that is expected will be delivered.

There is a large collection of the Winnebagoes at the Portage; Mr. Kinzie says about four thousand souls. They will be paid their annuity money on the first of July. Man Eater and the Indians of the Upper Rock river were all at the Portage. They are now camped on the Menominee lands, and say they have a right to remain. I think to remove the Rangers immediately from the frontier, many of the Winnebagoes will cross the Wisconsin below the Portage and return toward the Rock river.

I would have remained at the Portage with the Rangers until the annuity money was paid, and would have seen the Winnebagoes move across the Wisconsin, but the scarcity of supplies at Fort Winnebago obliged me to march the Rangers to Helena, where our supplies had arrived about the 18th inst.

I am strengthened in my belief that the Indians will return to the Rock river from the statements of Mr. Marsh, an agent of the American Fur Company. He called to see me, and stated to me that the fur trade of the Upper Rock river was worth twenty thousand dollars annually, that he had been

engaged in that trade about ten years; he appeared to regret much that the
Winnebagoes should be deprived of the privilege of hunting on the ceded
country, because the Pottawattamies would cross over their boundary and hunt
and trap on the ceded country. I stated to him I understood commissioners
had been appointed to treat with the Pottawattamies in September for their
country bordering on the State of Illinois. He said the Pottawattamies would
sell their country and were willing to move west of the Mississippi, but that
their crop of corn would be ripe in September, and that they could not remove
their corn with them, and that they would necessarily remain until spring,
which would give them the advantage of hunting in the Winnebago country
during the winter. Mr. Marsh has a wife and children among the Winnebagoes. Several of the Winnebago chiefs have applied to me for permission to
return to hunt on the ceded lands, which I have positively denied them.

I met Mr. Rolette near the Portage on my return, who informed me of the
order Col. Taylor had received as to the marching of the Rangers to the Sioux
and Chippeway country, and appeared much interested in the contemplated
movement up the Mississippi. The American Fur Company to which he is
attached is no doubt greatly interested that peace should be preserved between
the respective Indian nations with whom they have intercourse. This trader
has been deeply interested in the Rock river trade.

I think the proper course would be to range the country bordering on the
Wisconsin from Helena to the Portage until the term for which the Rangers
are enlisted expires. I have made an arrangement with Col. Cutler, commanding officer at Fort Winnebago to send me an express immediately should
the Winnebagoes not cross the Wisconsin. He thinks it would be improper
for them to remain on the lands of the Menomonees. Under my orders I
should consider I was bound to remove them across the Wisconsin. To permit them to remain on the lands of the Menomonees would facilitate their
immediate return to the Rock river country.

Capt. Beekes enlisted the greater part of his company on the 7th of July.
Their time would expire on the march to the Sioux and Chippeway country.
The time of enlistment of Capt. Browne's company would expire about three
weeks after that time. From the disposition already evinced by the Rangers
of Beekes's company, Col. Taylor would find it difficult to do anything with
them. Capt. Browne's company appear satisfied, and I think there would be
no difficulty with them.

DODGEVILLE, July 14th, 1833.

General H. Atkinson:

I ordered the Rangers to range the country carefully, and to take all straggling Indians they might find within the limits of the ceded country, and
retain them in safe keeping until further orders. From a conversation I had
with Daugherty and Mack, two Indian traders on Rock river, I suspected
them for secretly advising a part of the Winnebagoes to return to Rock river.
The Indian wife of Daugherty is the relation of Whirling Thunder, the principal chief of the Rock River Indians.

Whirling Thunder, his family, with several men (the party of Winnebagoes was composed of about twenty, including children) were found on Sugar creek, where they had camped. Daugherty had furnished his wagon to transport the baggage of Whirling Thunder and his party. A white man by the name of Davie was drawing the wagon with two Frenchmen; Emmell and another (his name I do not know) were in company. They were taken with Whirling Thunder and his party by Lieut. Wheelock of the U. S. Rangers, under the orders of Capt. Beekes, and conducted to the camp of the Rangers near the Four Lakes. I was immediately notified by express, and repaired without delay to the Four Lakes where I found the Indians and the three white men under guard. I released the whites, and sent Lieut. Fry, of the U. S. Rangers, with fifty men as an escort to guard Whirling Thunder and his party to the Portage, and cross them over the Wisconsin river.

In my conference with the Winnebagoes at the Portage, I discovered a desire on the part of the Winnebagoes to hunt on the lands of the Menomonees on Fox river. I suspected them for occupying that country only for the moment and then passing to the Upper Rock river. The Winnebagoes and Menomonees appear very friendly at present, and I have thought it probable there might be a secret understanding between them to that effect. Pauquette, the interpreter at the Portage, with whom you are acquainted, appears to think, unless the Winnebagoes are permitted to hunt on the lands of the Menomonees there will be difficulty between them, unless the latter nation is prevented from hunting on the lands of the Winnebagoes.

The Rangers commanded by Capt. Beekes, whose term of service expired, as they state, on the 7th of July, presented themselves forty-two in number, and demanded of the captain their discharge, stating they could only be compelled to serve the U. S. twelve months from the date of their enlistment, not from the time they were mustered by the inspecting officer into service. These men commenced stacking their public arms immediately before the tent of the captain, mounted their horses, and started for Indiana. A part of the balance have left the service in the same manner since, leaving not more than twenty men in Capt. Beekes' company, with two First Lieutenants, one Second Lieutenant, and two Brevet Lieutenants. Capt. Beekes applied to me for a furlough to return to Indiana; he has had a severe attack of the rheumatic pains, and is at present unfit for service. I granted him a furlough of sixty days.

The term of time for which Capt. Browne's men have been enlisted, upon the principle contended by the Rangers of Capt. Beekes' company, will expire in a few days, and should they discharge themselves in the same manner that Capt. Beekes' men left the service, this will leave the frontier without mounted men. Capt. Browne has two First Lieutenants, one Second Lieutenant, one Third Lieutenant, and one Brevet Lieutenant attached to his company; there will be eleven officers in both companies.

Under the General Order of the 11th of March the Mounted Rangers were held in readiness for active service until relieved by the Regular Cavalry. Under that Order I felt myself bound not to discharge the Rangers until I received orders to that effect. Had the country been in a state of war with the Indians, I should have taken stronger grounds. I think, however, a mounted force should be kept on this frontier, and that something should be done with the Indian traders who urge the **Indians to violate** their treaties with the U. S. If we have trouble on this frontier, it will be more the fault of the traders than the Indians; the large amount now to be paid the Winnebagoes makes their trade valuable; these traders are generally married to Indian women, and they always exercise an improper influence over the minds of the Indians.

Will you have the goodness to direct the disposition I shall make of the officers under my command on this frontier, should the Rangers discharge themselves.

July 15th, 1833.

General Atkinson:

I regret to inform you that the cholera has made its appearance in the camp of the Rangers near the Wisconsin. Yesterday two privates of Capt. Browne's company died in a few hours after their attack, and the Captain informs me there are several men who have the premonitory symptoms of this disease. I have sent an express for Dr. Phileo, and, if it is not in his power to come to our assistance, to send Dr. Crane. Dr. McLaren is a good young man, and no doubt a good physician, but has had no experience in this terrible disease.

I wrote you by the mail yesterday fully; this letter is sent by the express who is the bearer of my letter to Dr. Phileo.

Early in August Col. Dodge closed the work of the U. S. Rangers upon the Northwestern frontier, leaving a small detachment of thirty-five men upon the ground, whose term of service had not expired, under the following order:

NORTHWESTERN FRONTIER, August 7th, 1833.

Second Lieutenant James Clyman,
Commanding a Detachment of U. S. Rangers:

You will remain in the neighborhood of Dodgeville with the detachment under your command; your supplies of rations will be issued by Third Lieutenant John G. McDonald, until the first of October, at which time you will discharge the men of your detachment, unless sooner discharged by the order of Brigadier General Atkinson. You will once in two weeks range the country from your camp near Dodgeville to the Four Lakes, where you will be able to get information as to the movements of the Winnebagoes. Should you find any of them you will treat them friendly, and take no step that could possibly involve the frontier inhabitants in difficulty with the Indians; but should you ascertain that the Winnebagoes are returning to the lands they have ceded the United States, you will without delay report the facts to General Atkinson at Jefferson Barracks, or myself, should I be stationed at that place.

While occupied with the organization of the regiment of Dragoons at St. Louis, his brother, Dr. Linn, was called to St. Genevieve by the earnest entreaties of his old friends in that place, where there was a virulent outbreak of cholera.

In ministering to them Dr. Linn was himself seized with the epidemic, and anticipating a fatal result, he despatched a messenger for his wife, who was at St. Louis, to come to him. She immediately hurried on her way, driving down on the Illinois side of the river, and crossing the river again at St. Genevieve, in imminent peril in the darkness of the night, when she found her husband still living, and that hopes were entertained of his recovery. Soon after she had left St. Louis, Col. Dodge was advised of it, and he hastened to overtake her, but she was too swift in her journey. On reaching St. Genevieve the next morning, he told Mrs. Linn that he had frequently overtaken Indians running from him with all the fleetness for which they are remarkable, but he should never again try to overtake a wife flying to seek a sick husband. He had left St. Louis half an hour after her, and although mounted on a fine horse had tried in vain to overtake her.[1]

---

[1] Life and Public Services of Dr. Lewis F. Linn, by Mrs. E. A. Linn and Nathan Sargent, pp. 72-77.